THE INVASION OF SANDY BAY

THE INVASION OF SANDY BAY

Anita Sanchez

CALKINS CREEK
Honesdale, Pennsylvania

LIBRARY OF CONGRESS CATALOGING-IN-PUBLICATION DATA
Sanchez, Anita.
The invasion of Sandy Bay / Anita Sanchez. — 1st ed.
p. cm.
Includes historical notes.
Includes bibliographical references.
ISBN-13: 978-1-59078-560-7 (hardcover : alk. paper)
1. United States—History—War of 1812—Juvenile fiction.
2. Sandy Bay (Mass.)—History—19th century—Juvenile fiction.
[1. United States—History—War of 1812—Fiction.
2. Sandy Bay (Mass.)—History—19th century—Fiction.
3. Adventure and adventurers—Fiction.] I. Title.
PZ7.S19476Inv 2008
[Fic]—dc22
2007051224

CALKINS CREEK
An Imprint of Boyds Mills Press, Inc.
815 Church Street
Honesdale, Pennsylvania 18431

for Alex
and
for Timothy

Map by Joan Jobson

THE INVASION OF SANDY BAY

CHAPTER 1

September 8, 1814

Lemuel Brooks peered over the side of the wooden boat into the midnight water of Sandy Bay. He pulled cautiously on his fishing line and felt an answering tug. "Finally got something!" he whispered and twitched the line harder. He could feel the moving power in the water deep below.

Bill Tarr, in the rower's seat, shook his head. "That's no way," he scolded. "Give a good yank to set the hook." The old fisherman peered into the depths as eagerly as the boy. The sea was as clear as glass, and a silver gleam flickered below the little boat.

Lemuel swallowed, then took a deep breath and jerked on the rope. Instantly, the line went rigid, cutting through the water as the bristly rope burned his fingers.

"Put your back into her!" Bill ordered. Lemuel dropped the clumsy wooden reel and hauled in the dripping line hand over hand till his fingers were numb and his shoulders ached. A gray shape was rising through the darkness, and he grinned with excitement, craning his neck over the side. The fish was as long as his arm.

Bill rolled his eyes. "It's a fish, not the Reverend, boy—no need to tip your hat to it. Grab it by the gills!"

Lemuel reached eagerly into water so cold that it scalded his fingers. As soon as he touched the slimy scales, the fish gave a frantic lunge. Icy spray struck his face like hail, and the line went slack. He leaned far out to make a last desperate grab, but disappointment flooded him as the fish went glimmering down into the shadows.

A wave slapped the side of the dory and water surged over the low edge of the boat. "Good Lord, trim her!" Bill cried. "Don't you have the sense God gave a goat?"

Lemuel's stomach heaved as the boat lurched back and forth. He clutched both sides of the cramped little craft, taking care to shift his rump to the center of the narrow seat.

"I told your mother that twelve was too old to begin fishing," Bill grumbled. "Why, I was three years old the first time my grandfather took me—you act like you've never been in a boat before."

"Well, I haven't," Lemuel snapped. He knew he should always show respect to his elders, but his fingers were aching from the water's bitter chill.

Bill stared, pushing back his old-fashioned tricorne hat. "Do you mean to say," he said, drawing out each word, "do you mean to sit there and tell me ... that a lad your age has *never* been in a boat?"

Lemuel shook his head. "My father helped me make a raft for the mill pond one time ...," he began, then his voice faded. He wriggled on the hard seat while Bill chewed on the stem of his pipe, shaking his head.

"Well, it was only a twenty-pounder," Bill remarked finally with a shrug. "That was a fish, that was," he added. "Ever see one before?"

Lemuel snorted. "I've smelled them, anyhow," he muttered. The endless round of chores in the taproom, which had seemed so dull only yesterday, was looking better and better. Perhaps fishing was not his trade after all.

He cast a longing look over his shoulder at the hills of Cape Ann, dense black humps that rose against the lighter blackness of the sky. Across the wide darkness of the bay, the shore lights were as small as fireflies. A faint needle of white was just visible against the sky: a tall church spire, high on a hill. The small cluster of houses bore the same name as the rocky, wide-mouthed inlet that was so full of fish: Sandy Bay.

A pale red square marked where a lamp burned in a window. He knew his mother was waiting for him, probably looking out over the black water with a worried frown.

"Why do we have to go out in the middle of the night?" Lemuel asked. "At least in the daytime we could see where we were going, and then ..."

"Cod bite better when it's dark," snapped Bill, "and when it's quiet! Hush your noise and get your hook baited." The old man plunged his hand deep into the bait bucket for a piece of clam, thrust a three-inch hook through the smelly chunk, and handed Lemuel the reel. "Lower away, lively, now."

Lemuel wrinkled his nose as he dropped the lead-weighted line with a plop that sounded loud in the stillness. Widening rings disturbed the water's quiet surface. "Did you ever hear of the Cape Ann sea serpent?" Lemuel asked uneasily. "My father used to say that—"

"Stow your gab!" Bill ordered, and Lemuel shot the old fisherman a resentful glance. Lemuel lowered the hook for what seemed to be miles, until Bill finally grunted. Silence fell, broken only by the murmur of the breakers on Bearskin Neck and a faint hiss as Bill sucked on his pipe, making the embers glow.

The boat rocked in a monotonous rhythm, and Lemuel sat trying not to think about his cold, wet feet. The line hung limp in his hand, but Bill casually pulled in fish after fish. Soon there was a twitching pile of cod around their ankles, moonlight glinting on the bronze and silver scales.

Bill straightened from bending over his line and put a hand to his back as he shifted on the wooden seat. The old fisherman squinted around the black expanse of the bay, glancing back and forth with pursed lips, as though deciding which fork to take in a well-traveled road.

"Time to go back in?" Lemuel inquired hopefully.

Bill snorted. "We'll try out by Halibut Point next," he announced. "It's not more than a couple of miles."

"A couple of *miles*?" Lemuel wailed. Wisps of fog were beginning to rise from the icy water's surface like steam from a boiling pot. He eyed the faraway pinpoints of the shore lights. "What if it gets so foggy we can't see the land?" he asked. "Even the stars aren't out."

"Breakers on the Neck will guide us in," said Bill casually.

Lemuel peered into the dark. He could just make out a faint line of white where the waves met Bearskin Neck, a long and narrow arm of rock that jutted far into the wide bay. The waves surged forward against the wind, moving toward the land under their own power; he could hear the crash as each wave broke like splintering glass when it met the wall of granite. Lemuel shivered, realizing that there was barely an inch of planking between him and the deep water.

"What would happen if the boat, um ... tipped over?" Lemuel inquired. He tried to sound unconcerned, but there was a quaver in his voice.

"Why, what the sea wants, she'll take," Bill Tarr said. "No point worrying about every little thing, like an old hen." The oarlocks groaned as he began to row.

Lemuel clung to the hard wooden seat. "I'm not worried," he protested. "But if we didn't go too far out we could swim back, maybe, if the boat tipped over ..."

Bill snorted. "Swim! No Sandy Bay fisherman learns how to swim. Why, he'd be a Jonah, for sure."

"What's that?" asked Lemuel, watching the shore lights fade into the darkness.

"Bad luck," said Bill in a low tone. "A Jonah's anything that's right bad luck—could be anything, a bucket or an oar ... or a fellow that knows how to swim."

Lemuel thrust a hand in his pocket and groped among the litter of string, crumbs, and other debris for his lucky stone. He clutched it tightly.

"Don't worry, we'll find the way home." Bill's pipe wagged

under his swooping white mustache as he talked. "Can't miss on a calm night like this, sea's as smooth as milk. Wait till the wind's howling like a dog and the stars are gone. They should have built a lighthouse on the Neck instead of that blasted fort."

"Mr. Pool was saying they'll never build a lighthouse," Lemuel said. "Taxes so high already, with the war and all ..."

"The war—damned politicians' war." Bill spat over the side of the boat. "Cod down to two dollars a quintal, by God, two dollars for a hundred pounds of fish. Why, it used to be twice that!" He gave a vicious yank on the oars and rowed on.

Clouds were reaching up from the land to erase the moon and stars. Lemuel felt a stab of fear at losing sight of the homeward way. "Isn't this far enough?" he asked, but Bill shook his head and kept rowing, his head thrust forward on the end of his long, wrinkled neck like a tortoise.

Finally, Lemuel spoke again. "How much farther do we ...?"

"This is the spot," Bill interrupted, and Lemuel ground his teeth. Everyone interrupted him: his mother, the schoolmaster, the other boys—and it looked as if life in Sandy Bay wasn't going to be any different. No one was ever interested in what he had to say.

He brushed the hair out of his eyes and looked around uneasily at the vast, empty space, barren of any landmark. Tentacles of mist reached toward the boat.

"Bit of a fog tonight, but it'll clear by morning," Bill observed, cocking his head at the blank sky.

"Looks like rain to me," Lemuel retorted.

"It fair beats me how a lad as old as you don't know the first thing about the weather," Bill said. "Don't farmers know when it's going to rain?"

Lemuel heaved a sigh that came right up from his toes. He had lived on a small farm, ten miles inland, until only last month, but now it seemed as though he could hardly remember a time when "farmer" wasn't an insult.

Bill rebaited his line to the accompaniment of a steady, low grumble. "Fish're hardly worth the trouble of catching these days, with this cursed war that the idiots in Washington have wished on us." He tossed the hook over the side, letting the tough cord slide smoothly between his gnarled fingers. "Why, we fought the British already, by God! I was one of the lads that marched off to Bunker Hill, thirty-nine years ago this spring ..."

Lemuel leaned forward eagerly. A good yarn might take his mind off the cold darkness. But Bill's story meandered, pausing often to dwell on his bunions and the shoes that wore out during the march. Lemuel's mind began to wander, too, and he shivered. A sharp breeze was rising. He wished now that he'd taken his mother's advice about wearing his wool cap.

"Well, there'll never be enough money for a lighthouse, Mr. Pool says." Lemuel interrupted Bill, for a change. "And the town needed a fort. The war might go on for years."

Bill snorted. "Can't talk sense into landsmen anyhow. What do they care about a lighthouse?" He glanced seaward, where the sky met the water in an unbroken sweep of black. "Not that it matters, boy. What the sea wants, she'll take, you know. She'll take it when she wants it."

A faint, muffled creak drifted out of the quiet fog. Bill

frowned and leaned forward. The pipe embers glowed as he sucked in his breath. The creak came again: a small sound, like a door opening.

"What's the matter?" Lemuel whispered. The sea serpent stirred again in his mind.

"I don't know," Bill said slowly. "Hush." Again Lemuel heard it—a creak and then a groan. Both of them stared out over the rippling waves.

At first Lemuel could see only the woolly blackness. Then part of the darkness took shape and moved across the water toward them. As it loomed closer, the outlines of sails and masts appeared, and the high sides of a deck. A ghostly ripple glowed white about her bow.

"It'll run us down!" Lemuel cried. The approaching vessel slashed through the waves, headed directly for them, like a whale opening its jaws for a minnow. Bill gave a tremendous yank at the oars. Lemuel held his breath as the big ship neared, the pointed bowsprit stabbing overhead.

Then a high deck was gliding past like a shadowy cliff. Wind hissed in the rigging. A cannon mouth gaped wide, and then another; one by one a long row of ugly black guns passed, a yard away from his nose. Waves surged backward, and the dory wallowed like a drowning man.

"Bail, you fool!" shouted Bill, straining at the oars. Lemuel hastily grabbed a bucket and started tossing water over the side. The ship faded into the fog, silent as an owl.

Gradually the waves subsided. The bucket fell from Lemuel's numb fingers. Freezing water sloshed about his ankles. "That was a warship!" he said in a shaking voice. "Did … did you see the cannons? Think it was one of ours?"

Bill shook his head, scowling after the vanished ship. "British," he said. "Frigate, thirty guns or more." He swallowed. "Looking for boats to steal, the damned Limeys, and honest fishermen to press into their blasted navy."

"We should go back and tell someone!" said Lemuel. "That was close."

"Let's get out of here—" Bill stopped, his head tilted sharply.

The creak came again, followed by the muffled sound of shouted orders. Lemuel and Bill stared at each other with round eyes. Then they gazed into the fog, both of them leaning forward, listening, listening without daring to breathe.

The creak and rustle grew louder. The white gleam of sails took form through the mist.

"Sweet Jesus," Bill whispered. "She's coming around."

CHAPTER 2

The warship took shape in the gloom, slowing to a glide as the flapping sails were furled with a rattle and clatter. The tops of the great masts were hidden in the fog. Gilded carving decorated the frigate's bow and stern, just visible through the streamers of mist, and Lemuel spelled out the curving gold letters of her name: *Nymph.*

Along the side was a row of square doors from which jutted grim cannon mouths. In the misty moonlight, he could just make out a line of muskets poked over the side. Every one of the long barrels was aimed right at him.

This could not be happening. He would wake up soon in his little room under the eaves of the tavern, with his mother scolding him to get busy with the kindling and start the kitchen fire. But the ship was all too real; small waves slapped against its wooden side, and a strong smell, of tar and onions mixed with tobacco, wafted from the deck. The muskets pointed unwaveringly at his chest.

A harsh voice came from above: "You in the boat! Heave to, and come alongside. Sharply, now!"

Bill maneuvered his boat close under the dark cliff of the frigate as the bristling row of muskets followed their every move.

A rope snaked down from overhead. "Tie up your vessel," barked the voice, and Bill reached for the rope. His hands were shaking, and it took him three tries to fasten the knot that bound the dory to the enemy ship.

"Come aboard," came a final brusque order as a rope ladder with wooden steps clattered down toward them from the gloom above.

Bill's chin was trembling under his whiskers, but he clenched his jaw and took a deep breath, squaring his shoulders under his patched coat. He grasped the ladder and climbed upward as nimbly as a long-legged spider, clambered over the deck rail, and disappeared.

Lemuel sat alone in the dory, which now felt like an old familiar friend. He stared at the rolling side of the frigate and the dangling ladder swaying to and fro, till the motion made him feel queasy.

"Come aboard!" repeated the gruff voice above. "You there, boy. Move!"

He took a deep breath, as Bill had, gave the lucky stone in his pocket a quick rub, and stood up. The little dory gave a sudden toss, and he found himself sitting on the slimy pile of fish. Bill's pipe was floating upside down in the water that sloshed in the bottom of the boat.

Lemuel crawled out of the cold puddle, grabbed the ladder, and pulled himself up, setting a foot on the lowest rung. His other foot left the security of the boat as he swung out over the water with a sickening lurch. He managed to get a toehold on the next rung and inched his way up the swaying ladder, his teeth chattering. Finally he reached the deck rail, climbed over it, and landed on the deck with a thump.

He sat for a few seconds, panting, with tightly closed eyes. But no firing squad approached; nothing happened. There was no sound except a confused blur of voices. He opened his eyes cautiously and looked around.

A lantern swung from a bracket, lighting the deck and glowing on a forest of ropes. There seemed to be ropes everywhere: ropes as thick as his arm that reached from the sides of the deck up into the fog; ropes in a knotted tangle overhead; ropes twisted in tight coils like snakes.

Barefooted sailors were perched like gulls on the hatches and lined up in the rigging. A mast rose from the deck like an enormous tree, and in front of it clustered officers in long-tailed coats and cocked hats. All eyes were on a man who stood in the center of the little group. Plainly, this was the captain.

He was a small figure, shorter than most of his officers, but the epaulets on his blue coat widened his shoulders, and his high cocked hat was richly decorated with lace. The lantern light glittered on the rows of gold buttons on his chest. His face was stern, and his pale eyes ignored everything but the bent fisherman standing before him.

Bill Tarr stood, hands on hips, scowling at the captain. "So you think you've got us, hey?" Bill demanded. "Think you're pretty clever, hey? You'll never press us into your damned navy."

This speech had a familiar ring, and Lemuel realized that it was a line, or pretty close to it, from one of his father's stories:

the scary one about Nathan Hale, when the British were about to hang him. He could hear his father's voice, ringing out in the quiet kitchen, as the hero defied the enemy. Lemuel scrambled to his feet, wet shoes squelching. "We'll never join the Royal Navy," he declared, but his voice quavered. No one glanced his way.

The captain ignored Lemuel as he looked the ragged fisherman up and down. "Oh, His Majesty's not that hard up for seamen," he assured Bill. The crowd of sailors snickered and elbowed each other, grinning. "We require only a service of you, old man," the captain said sternly. "Then we'll let you go."

Bill's jaw dropped. "What!" he shouted. "I'm not good enough for the Royal Navy? I'll have you know I was sailoring before you could walk, young fellow. Why, I can pull twice the weight of these young jackanapes here ..."

"Well, if you're anxious to join up, perhaps we could accommodate you," said a blue-coated officer at the captain's elbow. "We can always use a few more powder monkeys."

"Quiet, Mr. Briscoe," the captain said. His eyes aimed straight at Bill. "We require only one service," he repeated. "And then you can be on your way."

"A service?" asked Bill, glaring up at the captain under bristly eyebrows. "And what might that be?"

"These are shoal waters, and I don't care to risk my vessel. I want you to pilot us into Sandy Bay."

Bill raised his whiskered chin and straightened his back. "Go to hell."

Lemuel gasped. The punishments that the British navy

meted out were well known. He had often shivered at the stories of captive American seamen being keelhauled or flogged with the dreaded cat-o'-nine-tails.

The captain made no reply, but the tall officer at his side took a swift step forward. "Keep a civil tongue in your head!" he ordered. "Or you'll find yourself swimming home."

The captain ignored this interruption. "Think it over," he said to Bill. "I give you my word of honor, and I never broke it in my life, that if you do not pilot my ship safely into Sandy Bay, you and the lad will go directly over the side."

The shadows tilted around the old man and the captain as the lantern swayed with the movement of the vessel. *"The lad?"* thought Lemuel, and then his stomach took an extra heave. "The lad" meant him.

He almost opened his mouth to shout defiance, as one of the heroes in his father's tales would surely do, but the thought of the lightless depths and the cold seawater made him shudder. He held his tongue.

The silence lengthened, broken by the creaks and groans of the drifting vessel. Finally, Bill glanced at Lemuel, then looked down at the deck and cleared his throat. He mumbled something, and gave a short nod.

"Very well," said the captain. He pointed to the bow. "Go forward, my man, and give us good warning of any reefs."

Bill turned and shuffled away, head down, avoiding all eyes. Lemuel let out the breath he had been holding. His surge of relief was mixed with a sour feeling of disappointment. A story wasn't supposed to end this way.

The captain turned to the lanky officer beside him. "Very well, Mr. Briscoe," he remarked. "We'll proceed slowly, but I think the fog's breaking up a bit. Douse all lights."

"Aye, sir," said the officer, saluting with a stiff palm. He shouted instructions to the crew, and a half-dozen sailors with black, tarred pigtails scrambled up into the rigging, clinging with bare toes to the web of ropes. They ran along the yard-arms, high overhead, and bent to tug at the knots that secured one of the sails. Lemuel watched with the same envy he felt for the Sandy Bay boys who flitted through the rigging of the fishing schooners in the harbor.

The fog was thinning; the long, fluttering pennant at the top of the mainmast was visible now. The sail flapped, then bellied out smoothly as it caught the gentle breeze. The deck moved like a great animal under his feet as the ship surged forward.

Lemuel staggered, and a hand caught his arm and steadied him. "Take it easy there, mate," said a deep voice. A tall, stocky man grinned down at him. A few teeth were missing from the grin. "Got to get your sea legs, there, Yank. Takes a bit of getting used to."

Lemuel jerked his arm away. He retreated till his back was pressed against the deck rail, and stared at the man's broad shoulders outlined against the night sky. The stranger wore a long-tailed coat that flapped unbuttoned over white breeches. In the moonlight the coat looked gray, but by day it would surely gleam scarlet: this must be a Lobsterback, a Limey—a Redcoat—the feared and hated enemy in all the best stories.

The man said something in his unfamiliar accent.

"What?" Lemuel asked. He grasped the rail, ready to dodge if the man should try to grab him again.

The man repeated his question. "You one o' them fishin' blokes, mate?"

"No," Lemuel said warily.

"Just out a-boatin' for your 'ealth, then, eh?" the man inquired. "It's a pleasant night for it."

"Well, I'm learning the trade," Lemuel admitted. "My mother runs a tavern, but I hate being a tavern keeper, so I have to learn another honest trade."

"Ah, a tavern," said the man, nodding as he scratched his broad stomach. "That'd be a fine place to live. But most innkeepers are tight-fisted sorts, I have to say, won't pour so much as a drop on tick."

"On what?"

"On tick—on credit, y'know. Your mother ever give credit, now?"

"Sometimes," said Lemuel, wondering if this was all some kind of trick.

"Well, what about your dad?" inquired the soldier. He sat down on a coil of rope, apparently prepared to chat all night. "He ever let an honest soldier have a drop on account?"

"My father died a few years ago," said Lemuel gruffly. He tried for a moment to imagine his father in a tavern, and failed. His father was forever in the farmhouse kitchen, reading in the rocking chair, waiting for Lemuel to come home from school.

The soldier frowned with heavy black brows, and his broad face looked grave. "Why, I'm sorry to hear that," he said solemnly.

"We moved to the tavern because my mother couldn't make the farm pay," Lemuel said, and sighed.

The flapping of the sails filled the awkward silence. "Ah, well," the stranger went on in a hearty tone, "that sounds a bit of an improvement over a farm, really, a nice snug tavern. Farm's a bloody lot of work, I've found. I'd be happy as a mouse in cheese in a tavern."

"Stop boring on forever about the tavern, Archer!" Another man approached, a small figure, wiry and sharp-nosed. The two white belts that crossed on his chest stood out even in the dim light. "I don't give a hang about the tavern," growled the newcomer. "I hear there's a good-size fort at Sandy Bay. That true, lad?"

Lemuel hesitated, reluctant to reveal military secrets to the enemy, but then nodded.

"That's why the old man's got his eye on this town," said the man glumly. "He's thinking that such a big fort must mean good pickings. "

"Lot of vessels in the harbor of a fishing town like that," said Archer. "Could mean prize money. That should please a tight-fisted sod like yourself, Martin."

"Aye, but the fort. I hear it's a very good-size fort," Martin persisted. "Brand new."

"Got any guns in there, then?" asked a new voice with a rough, burring accent. Lemuel turned and saw another soldier, a tall young man, with pale ginger-colored hair that blew in the breeze and the largest feet Lemuel had ever seen.

"Cannons?" said Lemuel. "Oh, yes."

The young soldier swallowed nervously. "How many?" he demanded.

"Dozens," said Lemuel promptly.

The soldiers glanced at each other, and the young man chewed his lip. His long, thin neck and gangly limbs were like the heron that stalked fish in the farm pond back home.

"And a whole regiment of Sea Fencibles," added Lemuel, beginning to enjoy himself a little. Since his arrival in Sandy Bay, he had often seen the smartly uniformed Sea Fencible militiamen in the drill yard by the church, marching up and down or busy with target practice. "They're garrisoned at the fort. And Colonel Appleton from Gloucester inspects the fort sometimes." He stood straighter as he repeated the name. "Colonel James Appleton."

"Old man's thinking of a sneak attack," observed Archer, eyeing the stiff, blue-coated figure of the captain across the deck. "That's why he wants to get in so close. It'll be us what has the honor of inspecting the fort tonight. His Majesty's Royal Marines."

"But you've got plenty of cannon on the ship here," Lemuel pointed out. "Won't the captain just open fire on the fort?"

"Haven't the wind with us tonight," said Martin, glancing up at the slow-moving clouds in the clearing sky. "We'd be a sitting duck if they returned fire." He spat over the deck rail. "We should try further up the coast," he complained. "It's crazy to try here."

"Aye, ye're the new admiral, eh?" said the ginger-headed young man "Ye'd better go and straighten out the old man, then—tell him he's daft, and ye've a better idea."

"I know what's what, Hill, that's all," Martin snapped. "We'll have trouble if we have to tack in this bay, with rocks God knows where. Bloody silly to build a fort there," he added. "Should have built a bloody lighthouse. Hope that old sod who's piloting us knows what he's doing."

They all turned toward the front of the ship, where Bill stood high on the bowsprit, flanked on each side by soldiers carrying muskets. Nearby stood a sailor who was dropping a weighted line over the side and monotonously chanting: "By the mark ten ... and a half nine ..."

"Bloody deep here, at least," observed Archer. "That's good."

Bill Tarr pointed to the left, and the barefooted sailor who stood behind the great wheel spun it hard. The ship heeled over. Lemuel lost his footing again, and Archer propped him up. "I haven't spent much time in boats," Lemuel confessed.

"Bloody queer fishermen they have in America," Martin remarked. "What d'you do, drop a line from the dock?"

"I'm not a fisherman," Lemuel retorted. "I'm from—"

"Look sharp!" Archer interrupted. "There it is."

Through the mist loomed low hills, and the pale line of breakers on Bearskin Neck. And there, on the end of the long peninsula, stood the brand-new fort: a hump on the end of the long arm of granite, like a clenched fist daring the British to come on.

The soldiers lined the deck rail, muttering among themselves. Lemuel followed and stood facing into the wind—he found the fresh air blowing in his face made his stomach feel better. He looked out over the water at the sleeping town.

Till tonight, the little fishing village had seemed a dull place, compared with the farm he had lived on all his life. Sandy Bay had no haylofts to hide in, no meadows to roam, none of the things that made life interesting. The boys of Sandy Bay had no time to spare for a farmer's son, and all they ever talked of was fishing: the tide and the weather and the supply of bait; catching fish and cleaning fish and drying fish. But now Lemuel gazed at the little town with new-found pride.

"Made of stone, eh?" inquired Archer, who leaned beside him on the rail.

"You bet," said Lemuel with relish. "Huge stone walls." This was quite true: the fort was constructed of granite blocks quarried from the hills behind the town and then carted with enormous labor along the length of Bearskin Neck. A square wooden watchtower peered over the ramparts.

"Bloody 'ell," said Martin, staring at the huge semicircle of rock. "Must be fifty feet wide. Stone, eh? Most towns have nothing but a big pile of dirt." Lemuel grinned in the darkness.

A lop-sided moon edged through the thinning clouds. The warm land breeze blew the last curtains of mist aside and revealed the rest of the town that lined the quiet bay. Fishermen's cottages huddled near the water, then a line of houses and shops straggled up a steep hill crowned with a blocky white tower. At the top of the tower, tall columns held a high, domed roof over a great bell.

Lemuel pointed, eager to show off his knowledge. "There's

the church," he said. "The Old Sloop, they call it, because it's as high as the mast of a sloop."

"Puts London to shame," Martin sniggered. "St. Paul's bleedin' Cathedral, right enough."

"It's more than three stories high," said Lemuel, annoyed.

Up at the bow, the captain was surveying the long peninsula of Bearskin Neck. His telescope was trained on a spot about halfway down the long, thin point of land, a little rock-bound harbor where dozens of fishing craft bobbed at their mooring stones. Near the harbor was a long, low building with a gabled roof: the Punch Bowl Tavern.

It was queer, Lemuel thought, to look at the shutters of his own bedroom window from the outside. He thought of the cozy little room and the crackling straw mattress, covered with a warm quilt. A blurry spot of gold showed that a light still burned in the tavern.

The water rose and fell on the rocks of Bearskin Neck with a sleepy rustle like the breathing of a giant. A gull gave a lonely call. "Awful quiet, isn't it?" said Archer in a low voice.

Lemuel frowned across the dark water at the fort. A garrison of Sea Fencibles was stationed there, as he had told the soldiers, armed with muskets and well-polished bayonets. There was supposed to be an alert Sea Fencible on sentry duty in the watchtower at all times. He waited for a shout from the fort or the crack of a musket, but no sound broke the stillness. The ship surged closer to the sleeping town.

"Caught napping!" a voice rasped in his ear, and he turned to see Bill Tarr at his elbow.

"Why don't they sound the alarm?" Lemuel demanded in a low voice.

"That gaggle of clam diggers?" Bill sneered. "They couldn't fight off a lobster. They're probably all snoring."

"You mean they're asleep?" Lemuel demanded in horror. "They couldn't be."

Bill snorted. "Isaac Dade and Amos Storey and that lot," he said. "They could sleep through a nor'easter. And Benjamin Haskell hasn't whipped 'em into shape—all he does is show off his new uniform in front of the girls."

"The ladies like a uniform, there's no doubt about it," observed Archer cheerfully.

Bill glared up at the big soldier. "Those lubbers could never have defended Bunker Hill," he pointed out. "Why, we had to march night and day for a week. ..."

His voice went on, but Lemuel had stopped listening. He glared at the mist-wreathed town, peaceful in the moonlight. Sandy Bay had never looked so much like home before.

His fists beat on the railing. "Wake up!" he whispered. "Wake up!"

CHAPTER 3

"Very well, men," the captain said in a low voice. The soldiers and sailors who crowded the rail turned at once to face him, leaving only Lemuel and Bill looking landward. "The colonials have quite a little fortification there," the captain observed calmly. "Let's have a closer look, shall we? Mr. Briscoe, take in all sail and drop anchor."

"Yes, sir, right away," said the officer, and drew in his breath to shout.

"Quietly, mind," the captain said sharply, and Mr. Briscoe turned his shout into a murmur. There was a series of muttered orders and a scurry of bare feet. The sailors crept into the rigging, and the sails were furled in silence, the white sheets glimmering in the night like ghosts. A rattle of chains made Lemuel jump. A splash sounded, and he saw weird green sparks of phosphorescent light flicker in the water as the anchor sank into the tar-black depths. The ship whispered to a stop and lay on the gentle waves.

All eyes turned to the captain, who stood drumming his fingers on the deck rail. "Mr. Briscoe," he said thoughtfully. "Let's see if we can spike those guns."

"Yes, sir," said the officer with a broad grin. Lemuel shot

an agonized glance at Bill, but the old man shrugged and sat down on a hatch, bowing his head.

"Tell the marines to turn out." The captain folded his telescope with a snap. "Mr. Hurley, a word, if you please."

"Yes, sir!" said a shrill voice, and a slight figure, no taller than Lemuel, stepped forward smartly. He was dressed like the soldiers in a red coat, but loops and swirls of gold braid decorated his sleeves.

"Lower away the landing barges, Mr. Hurley," said the captain. "And I'd be pleased to see how many of those fishing vessels you can capture. No whistles, mind, and tell Sergeant Archer to muffle the oars." He turned back and raised his telescope to the fort again as the officer hurried off.

The sea was still dark, but the sky was gray in the east. A warm land breeze sighed through the ropes that festooned the tall masts. Lemuel strained his eyes through the thinning fog, but there was still no sign of any guard in the watchtower, no sound from the fort.

The marines sat on barrels and coils of rope in the stern, checking the priming of their muskets. The mutter of conversation died as the young officer bustled up, buckling a sword belt around his waist. "Come on, lads, time to go," he ordered. The soldiers got to their feet promptly, but their low-voiced grumbling resumed as soon as he strode away.

"Time to earn our keep, boys," said Archer with a sigh. He got to his feet and straightened his scarlet coat. "What we took the King's shilling for. Button up, there, Hill, you look like a scarecrow."

"Aye," Martin added gloomily, fingering the white straps that crossed on his chest. "With a bloody great target right on the front."

"Spit!" Hill protested. "'Tis bad luck to mention ... ye know."

Pig-tailed sailors hauled on ropes to lower a long, flat barge over the side of the frigate. Lemuel hung over the rail and watched as the awkward craft hit the water with a smack. A short, stubby cannon jutted from the front of the barge.

The sailors cursed quietly, straining on the ropes as another barge was lowered on the other side of the ship. The marines lined up to descend into the boats. Their coats were beginning to show scarlet in the brightening dawn.

"Well, nice to make your acquaintance, mate," said Archer, holding out his hand to Lemuel. "Duty calls."

Lemuel shook the outstretched hand. "Good luck," he said, then snatched his hand away. "I mean ..."

Archer laughed out loud. "How many guns you really got in that fort, Yank?" he asked in a low voice.

Lemuel hesitated, then shrugged and told the truth. "Two."

Archer slapped him on the shoulder and joined the other figures moving across the deck. There were mumbled curses as the marines climbed awkwardly down the ladder, clutching their muskets. Lemuel stood amid the crowd of sailors that lined the rail. The boats moved away from the shelter of the big ship's sides, gliding toward the town.

Each boat had a dozen or so men bent over the oars and an officer in the stern, whispering orders. The oarlocks were muffled with rags so that the only sounds were creaks and small splashes. The boats stayed close together until they approached the tip of Bearskin Neck, where the white gleam of breakers warned of rocks. There the two craft parted company: one barge went around the far side of the Neck in the direction of the harbor, while the other boat headed toward the fort.

Lemuel dug his fingernails into the wooden rail. The warning that beat inside his head was bursting to be shouted aloud, but the noise of the breakers would certainly drown his voice. He gritted his teeth, looking down at the water, and in his desperation even considered swimming. If only there was some way to raise the alarm, some way to get to shore! The town seemed to be so close he could almost touch it. Even Bill's little dory could be rowed there in a few minutes.

The dory!

He had forgotten the little boat in the excitement. Ignored by the crew, he scuttled to the stern of the ship. Sure enough, the dory was there, still attached to the towrope, tagging behind the big ship like a puppy at the heels of a stallion.

He moved back toward the bow, careful not to run or draw attention to himself. An officer gave him a contemptuous glance, then returned his gaze to the still-silent shore. Officers and sailors were silhouetted against the brightening sky as they lined the rail, all their attention focused on the fort.

Lemuel sidled over to Bill, still slumped on the hatch cover, and bent to whisper in his ear. The fisherman shook his head, but Lemuel persisted, tugging at his jacket, and finally Bill raised his head. He eyed the backs of the enemies lining the deck and gave a ferocious snort. Rising stiffly to his feet, he tip-toed behind Lemuel to the stern rail, and together they peered over the side to where the dory floated far below.

"Think we could climb down that little rope?" Lemuel whispered, eyeing the slender towline that swayed in the breeze.

Bill sniffed. "Any sailor could," he said. "Don't know about a farmer." He spat on his palms and then threw a leg over the rail, muttering, "His Majesty's not that hard up for sailors, eh? I'll show His Majesty a trick or two." He grasped the rope and slid smoothly down, stepping lightly into the boat as it rose on a swell.

Lemuel spat in his hands, too, then grabbed the rope and let himself slide. "Ow!" he cried as the rope ran between his palms with a red-hot pain. He let go without meaning to and landed with a thud in the boat, making it bob and toss.

But for once Bill didn't complain about the clumsiness of landlubbers. In one smooth motion, the old man untied the rope that connected them to the ship, then grasped the oars and dipped them in the water without a splash. The dory slid away from the frigate's side.

There was no noise from the ship as the distance widened. "Think they'll shoot us?" Lemuel muttered, grasping the sides tightly.

Bill shook his head. "Not unless they want to wake up the whole town," he said. He pulled for the harbor while Lemuel turned away from the frigate and faced the land, trying not to think about possible muskets being aimed at his back.

They drew near the foaming breakers on the rocks of

Bearskin Neck, and the dory began to bounce. Bill ignored the white turmoil of the breaking waves and guided the boat with long-practiced ease through the currents that swirled around the peninsula. Lemuel strained his ears for any alarm from the fort, but all he could hear was the rumble and crash of the waves.

Finally, Bill rowed, panting, into the gap in the wall of rock where granite boulders guarded the entrance to the little town harbor. A forest of slender masts poked above the docks; there were boats of all shapes and sizes, from two-man rowboats like Bill's to the tall sloops and schooners that could hold a half-dozen fishermen. Bill hastily sculled between the boats and edged the dory next to the stone pier. He didn't pause to tie up, just scrambled up the ladder. Lemuel climbed up at Bill's heels, his feet slipping on the slimy seaweed that coated the lower rungs.

At the top of the ladder, Lemuel paused, expecting to see a troop of Royal Marines marching down Bearskin Neck. But the road was empty. The cottages and bait shacks that lined the Neck were silent, the windows shuttered.

"Come on!" Bill shouted, and Lemuel scrambled up the rest of the ladder and leaped onto the pier. This was more like it. This was the way his father's stories went—like the one about Paul Revere waking the Minutemen with the news of the British attack. For a moment, Lemuel remembered the cozy farmhouse kitchen, his father beginning the tale as his mother clicked her knitting needles.

Bill was loping down the rocky track that led to the center of town. Lemuel shook off the memory of the firelit kitchen and followed.

A stone's throw from the harbor, he passed a building with a sagging roof of low eaves and pointed gables. Over the door hung a faded sign that creaked in the wind; it read "Punch Bowl," with a bunch of grapes painted beneath. Lemuel cast a regretful look over his shoulder at the lighted window, but he kept going; there was no time to go in and reassure his mother now.

He soon passed the panting fisherman and raced on into Dock Square, a wide yard of bare, hard-packed dirt enclosed by small shops and houses. The square was deserted; no fishermen's wives worked the handle of the water pump this early in the morning, no children played marbles under the tall elms. The only sign of life was the usual row of seagulls perched on every roof, ruffling their feathers and peering down at him sleepily. The misty gray dawn made the familiar long-handled pump look like a soldier with musket and bayonet. Lemuel stood panting in the quiet space, wondering which door to pound on first.

Then Bill appeared from around the corner of the tavern and puffed into the square, his long legs moving stiffly. "What the devil are you waiting for?" he wheezed. "Come about! We'll start with Mr. Pool."

The old fisherman hurried toward a brick house that took up most of the seaward side of the square. The high windows and four tall chimneys were rimed with salt from the ocean wind. It was the biggest house in Sandy Bay, the newly built home of Ebenezer Pool, the leading member of one of the town's oldest families.

Bill trotted up the steep steps to the carved and painted door. He ignored the shiny brass knocker, just threw himself at the door and banged on it with both fists, shouting in his reedy voice. "British in the harbor! We're under attack! The British!"

No answer. Bill pounded again, shouting. Lemuel joined in. The gulls lined up on the crest of the roof began to flutter their wings and give their strange, wailing call.

Finally, a window was thrown open on the second floor. A young man wearing a nightcap thrust his head out and glared down at them. Lemuel almost didn't recognize his elegant neighbor; Mr. Pool usually wore a tall beaver hat and a frock coat with gold buttons.

"What on earth are you about?" shouted Ebenezer Pool. "Are you drunk again, Tarr?"

"Who d'you think you are, the Reverend?" demanded Bill. "I'm sober as a judge!"

"Then why are you waking honest folk out of their beds?" retorted Pool, preparing to slam the window down.

"The British are ...," Lemuel began, but Mr. Pool waved a hand. "Oh, wait a minute, wait just a minute," he said, yawning, and shut the window.

"Sweet Jesus!" Bill exclaimed, looking up to the heavens. "If ever a town deserved to be invaded!"

He banged on the door again. Lemuel hammered with the brass knocker, but the handle was jerked out of his grasp as the door popped open. Ebenezer Pool emerged onto the doorstep. His big frame was clad in a purple dressing gown, and his tousled red hair was covered by a nightcap. "Now what's all this fuss?" he demanded.

"The British are—," Lemuel began.

"Hush, boy," Bill snapped and poured out the tale while Lemuel tried to insert a word every few seconds. Pool listened, blinking.

When the story was finished, Ebenezer Pool frowned at them in silence, and Lemuel feared he would slam the door in their faces. The weird cry of the gulls sounded overhead. But the young man finally seemed to take in the shocking news.

"British, you say?" Pool said, drawing himself erect. "The British on our very doorsteps?" His face grew red. "I'll go and turn out the Sea Fencibles! Tarr, run and rouse Captain Haskell." He prodded Bill in the chest. "Quick, man, not a moment to lose! What the devil are you waiting for?"

"Wait!" pleaded Lemuel as the other two started down the steps. "What about me? What should I do?"

"Why, run to the church as fast as you can, boy!" Ebenezer Pool bellowed. "Go and ring the bell!"

CHAPTER 4

The first clang of the church bell splashed into the silent dawn.

Lemuel hauled on the bell rope, grimacing as the rope scrubbed his sore palms. He gritted his teeth and pulled harder, and overhead the bell boomed again. Surely no one could sleep through this!

The noise was making a satisfactory alarm, but in the echoing belfry, he had no idea what was going on outside. British troops could be marching up the hill right now, and he wouldn't be able to hear a thing. He gave one last yank on the bell rope, then ran down the winding stairs and stuck his head out a narrow window to see what was happening.

A strange smell overpowered the usual fishy aroma: a nasty odor of burning. The smell filled him with dismay. He looked out toward the sea, and sure enough, orange flames glared at the tip of Bearskin Neck. A thick column of smoke stretched high in the calm air, blurring the last traces of the stars. The wooden watchtower behind the fort was blazing like a torch.

At the bottom of the hill below the church, the townsfolk were gathering in Dock Square. The crowd swirled in confusion like the harbor waters at the turn of the tide: mothers dragged children by the hand, men shouted and argued, boys yelled, dogs barked—it was like the chicken coop back home on the night the fox got in.

Most of the Sandy Bay folk were still just a blur of faces to Lemuel; he and his mother had taken up residence in the tavern only a few weeks ago, and he was still sorting out who was who. He picked out a few familiar faces among those in the square: Tom Wheeler, a tall and burly fisherman who lived on the Neck, across the way from the Punch Bowl; Ebenezer Pool, still clad in his dressing gown and carrying a musket; Hezekiah Tarr, Bill's wife, a stooping figure in a black shawl.

A troop of elderly fishermen pounded down the hill toward the square. They were the ones, like Bill Tarr, who told stories of Bunker Hill in the tavern night after night; they wore pigtails and tricorne hats and brandished the same swords they had carried in their Minuteman days of forty years before.

All the boys in town had turned out. He recognized Caleb Tarr, one of Bill's numerous nephews, and the Norwood brothers—boys he had watched as they effortlessly rowed across the bay or swung through the rigging of their fathers' sloops. The boys whooped with excitement, all the roosters in town crowed, and the gulls circled over the hubbub, adding their voices to the din. Bill Tarr stood on the doorstep of the Pool house, pointing seaward and shouting.

From the high church window, Lemuel had a wide view of the ocean. The eastern sky was clearing as the morning wind blew strongly from the sea, and the fog had vanished into shreds of mist. A bright spark, like a sudden fire, showed over the edge of the horizon, as the rim of the sun appeared. The gold light outlined the tall ship that rode at anchor in the bay; the frigate's bare masts poked up into the pink sky, and the row of cannons was clearly visible along the sides.

Then Lemuel's jaw dropped in horror. Closer to land, just outside the harbor, a flat, low-slung barge was nearing the shore, crowded with men whose coats shone blood-red in the newly risen sun. A long black gun tilted up from the boat's bow.

The Sandy Bay folk were gathering at the water's edge. Some lined the stone piers of the harbor, others crowded onto the muddy strip of beach. Ebenezer Pool aimed his musket across the water, and a plume of smoke blasted out the long barrel of the weapon. Other men fired, and sparks flew over their heads with each crackling of shots.

Through the drifting smoke, he could see the soldiers in the barge busying themselves about the snout of the cannon. Then they all scrambled to the far end of the boat, except for one who stood directly behind the cannon, blowing on the orange gleam of a slow match. Lemuel strained his eyes; the smoke made it impossible to recognize the face, but the broad-shouldered man had a familiar look.

"Stop that!" Lemuel called. "Hold on a minute!" But the sea wind blew his words away. The soldier slowly lowered the bright torch toward the gun, and Lemuel held his breath.

A tremendous blast hit his ears like a fist. As the din echoed between the houses, pieces of grapeshot arced high overhead toward the crowd on the beach. Lemuel leaned so far over the narrow windowsill that he almost fell out, and he grabbed the sides of the window, expecting any moment to see Sandy Bay folk falling to the ground.

But the grapeshot spattered harmlessly into the bay, sending up fountains of white water. No one seemed to be injured. The crowd shook their fists; babies wailed and women screamed. The muskets cracked again.

Lemuel turned and took the steep stairs three at a time, back up to the small belfry. He yanked on the rope and grinned as he heard the brave defiance of the bell ring out overhead.

Then another explosion of cannon fire sounded, louder than the first. The boom reverberated in his chest like approaching thunder. From the dark tower above came a splintering crash. The bell clanged once more. Then, silence.

The bell rope went slack in his hand, like a fishing line when the cod has pulled free. He jerked at the rope frantically, but there was no sound. Cracks of daylight shone through the bell tower far above. He dropped the rope, saying every forbidden word that he had heard from the fishermen on the docks, and ran, slipping and stumbling, down the narrow stairs.

Splinters crunched under his feet as he came out into the road in front of the church. Shards of wood like giant toothpicks littered the ground. He turned, tilting his head far back to see how bad the damage was. The bell tower, tall as the mast of a ship, stood silhouetted against the pale sky. One of the slender white columns was shattered so that the domed roof leaned like a cocked hat. The bell hung unmoving. Lemuel kicked at a pile of debris, sending splinters flying.

There was no reason to stay in the deserted church, so he

turned and ran down the hill. A crowd of silent townsfolk stood on the beach, facing the invaders across the stretch of gray water. He elbowed his way to the front, shoving past night-capped fishermen, children, and women in shawls and nightgowns.

Foul-smelling cannon smoke hung low over the bay and drifted toward the shore. The British soldiers in the barge were shouting congratulations, slapping each other on the back and pointing up at the ruined bell tower. The sound of their laughter carried over the water with startling loudness. The soldiers began to pass another small black ball from hand to hand, and one of them, a tall, lanky soldier, hoisted it into the cannon mouth. The morning sun glinted on his ginger-colored hair.

A woman in a black knitted shawl stood near Lemuel—Mrs. Tarr, Bill's wife. Her hands were clasped as if she were praying, her wrinkled face creased in fear. But as the soldier raised his smoldering torch, she bent stiffly and picked up a piece of granite. She tossed it feebly, and the heavy rock fell far short of the mark.

She gave a determined snort, and bending down again, she hauled up her skirt. Balancing on one leg like an awkward seabird, she pulled off a long gray woolen stocking. Lemuel stared, thinking she had run mad.

She carefully looped the neatly darned stocking around a rock. "David slew Goliath with the power of righteousness!" she cried in a cracked voice. Using the stocking as a sling, she swung the rock overhead and heaved it far out into the bay. A white burst of spray splashed up close to the barge.

Other townsfolk picked up rocks, too. Lemuel grabbed a cold chunk of granite and hefted it, wondering if he could throw that far. The men raised their muskets. The red-coated soldier brought the torch closer to the barge's gun as a hailstorm of rocks flew toward the boat.

Lemuel stared at the enemy craft, measuring the distance; he drew his arm back, ready to hurl the rock. Then he hesitated. Something seemed strange about the way the barge floated on the calm water; surely the long flat shape had an odd tilt. He rubbed his tired eyes and looked again. He wasn't mistaken.

He pointed and began yelling at the top of his voice. "Look! Look at the boat!"

"What?" shouted Ebenezer Pool. He stood knee-deep in the water, his musket aimed at the barge. "What are you talking about?"

"The lad's right!" called Tom Wheeler, the black-bearded fisherman. "Look at her waterline, mates! She's down by the bow!"

Sure enough, the barge was tilting. The front end, weighed down by the heavy gun, was sinking visibly into the calm water.

"She's sprung a beam!" shouted Ebenezer. "The cannon's knocked a plank loose!"

"She's sprung, for sure," agreed Bill Tarr. "She's sinking!"

A burst of excited shouts went up from the Sandy Bay townspeople, young and old, man and woman. Standing on the muddy shore in their nightcaps, they watched with glee as the soldiers in the boat argued and cursed.

"Better start bailing, lads!" Tom Wheeler yelled across the water. The soldiers apparently obeyed and began to bail with frantic haste.

"Use your hats!" Bill advised shrilly as the soldiers flung water over the sides with their bare hands. But no matter how desperately they bailed, the barge continued to sink. The long muzzle of the gun disappeared into the water. Lemuel began to giggle.

Around him stood grizzled fishermen, boys in their night-shirts, ancient widows, pretty young girls; all began to smile, then to chuckle. Laughter rang across the bay, mingling with the curses of the soldiers. A roar of merriment arose from the shore as the red-coated invaders were gently deposited into the freezing waters of Sandy Bay.

CHAPTER 5

"Neighbors! Be calm!" A strong voice rose over the hilarity of the folk on the beach. "Is anyone injured?" A lone figure elbowed his way through the crowd; a tall man, not clad in nightshirt and cap like most of the townsfolk but fully dressed in a neat black suit. The long tails of his coat fluttered in the dawn breeze.

The laughter abated as people looked around at the new arrival. Some of the men looked sour, but they all took off their caps, and the women pulled their shawls tightly around themselves to hide their nightdresses. Lemuel recognized the tall figure at once: the Reverend David Jewett, pastor of the Old Sloop church. Lemuel had spent every Sunday since his arrival in Sandy Bay fidgeting on an uncomfortable pew, enduring the Reverend's two-hour sermons.

The Reverend's pale blue eyes surveyed the crowd, and Lemuel stepped behind a tall fisherman to avoid notice. Mrs. Tarr patted her wildly disheveled hair, gazing at the minister worshipfully. "Thanks be to God the Reverend's here!" she cried. "Now all's right."

"He hasn't brought a musket, but maybe he can preach 'em to death," muttered Bill.

His wife ignored him and hobbled up to the minister to clutch his sleeve with both hands. "Oh, Mr. Jewett, what's to be done?" she wailed. "It's a judgment, the ungodly coming with their cannons and their ships. What do they want of us peaceful folk?"

"They don't want anything," said Tom Wheeler, a grin showing through his black beard. "They're just trying to scare us."

Ebenezer Pool's round face was flushed. "They'll find out that's not so easy!"

"They that are unrighteous shall be punished," said Reverend Jewett. "But we must see what can be done here." He shook off Mrs. Tarr's grasp. "Is anyone injured?" he called again.

No one answered. Most of the townsfolk were still holding their sides and shouting with laughter. Lemuel looked out toward the sparkling bay, where there was nothing to be seen of the barge or the cannon; all that remained of the British assault force was a dozen or so heads bobbing a hundred yards from shore. The soldiers churned up white foam as they struggled in the deep water.

Lemuel slowly stopped laughing, and his grin faded as cries for help began to penetrate the townsfolk's noisy mirth. Like the Sandy Bay fishermen, the British soldiers knew that whatever the sea wanted, she would take. And so the Royal Marines had never learned to swim.

Footsteps pattered behind Lemuel, and he turned to find himself enveloped in his mother's embrace. Mrs. Brooks had pulled an old cloak over her nightgown and was wearing down-at-heel carpet slippers. Her red-brown hair had escaped from its usual tight knot and straggled down her back. She hugged him tightly, her ample bosom heaving; she was a stout lady, and her run down Bearskin Neck had made her mightily out of breath.

"Oh, thanks be to God!" she panted. "You've come safe home. When that cannon went off, I nearly fainted—are you all right, my poor darling?" She squeezed him again, her nightcap slipping off her untidy hair.

He pulled free, hoping none of the other boys had seen. "I'm fine, I'm fine," he said impatiently and turned back toward the bay where the soldiers splashed about, shading his eyes against the dazzle of the sun on the water. "Look out there!"

"Let them alone, wicked soldiers who come to kill us in our beds!" Mrs. Brooks cried.

The jeers and laughter faded as the fishermen and their families turned toward the water that shone a cheerful blue in the morning sun. The long skirts of the women flapped in the breeze from the sea. Many of them wore the black shawls of widows. The Sandy Bay folk stood in silent rows and watched the drowning men.

Bill Tarr stood on the shore, his seaboots in the water, his weathered brown face expressionless as he gazed at the soldiers who had captured them at gunpoint the night before. Lemuel remembered his words in the boat: *What the sea wants, she'll take.* The cries of the soldiers grew faint.

Lemuel ran to the water's edge, the cold water lapping over his shoes, and stood next to Bill. "They can't swim," he said urgently. "They'll drown!"

Bill Tarr glanced down at him. His eyes were almost hidden in the maze of wrinkles around them, but Lemuel caught a blue gleam. Then Bill began to smile. At first it was hard to see under the wiry whiskers that covered his upper lip, but then the grin spread across his face.

"I'll show His Majesty a trick or two," he muttered. Then he turned to wave his arm at the townsfolk. "Come on, lads," he cried. "Some nice big ones out there. Let's go fishing!"

There was a burst of applause from the crowd. Bill Tarr, Tom Wheeler, and a few other fishermen trotted over to a big dory that was pulled up on the beach. Hauling the boat into the shallow water, they waded alongside and hopped in.

"Heavens above, what a night!" cried Lemuel's mother. She pulled the threadbare cloak around her shoulders as they watched the men in the boat run out the oars. "It's a mercy we've not all been murdered, or blown to pieces. Come away home before they start that dreadful shooting again!"

She grasped his arm and began to urge him up the beach toward the tavern, but he tugged his arm free and watched eagerly as the dory drew near the soldiers. The fishermen pulled most of the British safely into the boat, while a few of the marines managed to splash their way toward the shore. The bedraggled soldiers were soon staggering up the beach, their scarlet jackets dripping. The rescue boat swiftly returned to the beach, and the keel grated on the rough shingle.

Lemuel, on the outskirts of the crowd, shoved forward to see who was being brought ashore. He spotted Hill, the lanky ginger-haired soldier, as Tom Wheeler grasped the boy by the scruff of the neck and dropped him on the sand. Other soldiers clambered awkwardly out of the boat, and Lemuel recognized a dripping, panting Martin; they were joined by Sergeant Archer, who waded ashore, hauling the young officer by the back of his coat.

The outnumbered soldiers huddled in a circle, facing outward with raised fists. The lieutenant crouched on the sand, gasping, his red coat streaming seawater. Archer bent and pulled the young officer to his feet, and they both stood, swaying.

The town boys assembled, at a safe distance from the enemy. Some of them came daringly close to the soldiers and began to point and jeer. Their shrill laughter grated on Lemuel's ears like the screaming of the gulls.

"Look at the Lobsterbacks!" shouted Caleb Tarr. He held his bony nose and pointed. "They smell as bad as last week's fish." He grabbed a piece of granite from the beach and hurled it at the soldiers. The rock caught Sergeant Archer on the shoulder with a thud, making him stagger.

The boy picked up another stone and drew back his arm.

"Stop that!" shouted Lemuel as he grabbed Caleb's sleeve.

Caleb gave him a shove. "Get out of this, farmer boy, go back to your plowing," he said.

"Stop it!" Lemuel insisted. "They're not ... I mean ... it wasn't their fault."

"Are you crazy?" demanded Caleb. "They burned the fort! And look at the church. You think it blew itself up?"

Lemuel gulped. "Well, they were just following orders. ..."

The boys elbowed each other, snickering. "What do you know about it, you landlubber?"

"I was there," said Lemuel stoutly. "I was on the ship." Caleb snorted, but Lemuel went on. "We were out fishing, and the British picked us up—captured us. Pointed guns at us and everything," he added with a touch of pride.

"Picked you up?" said Caleb. "What'd they want *you* for?"

"Wanted to make him admiral," shouted one of the boys. "Then they changed their minds and dropped him overboard."

"They did pick us up," insisted Lemuel. "They wanted someone to pilot them into the bay, to avoid the shoals. ..." His voice trailed off as all of the boys stared at him.

"Pilot them in?" repeated Caleb slowly. "And you did?"

"Well, I ... not me, exactly ... they had guns, you see. ..." Lemuel floundered.

"Get out of here, you traitor," Caleb sneered. His thin nose tilted upward with scorn.

The other boys echoed him. "Turncoat!"

"Benedict Arnold!"

And then the most deadly insult of all: "Farmer!"

Caleb picked up another rock and took aim at the group of shivering soldiers. Lemuel grabbed his arm, and the tall boy turned and shoved Lemuel in the chest. Lemuel staggered back and sat down on the muddy beach with a splat. The other boys picked up rocks and were poised to hurl them at the soldiers when a tall, black-clad figure swiftly strode up behind. Seizing Caleb by his collar and belt, he propelled the astonished boy headfirst into the water.

The dripping Caleb scrambled to his feet, cursing, but stopped when he saw who the newcomer was. All the boys stared in amazement. "Turn the other cheek, lads," Reverend Jewett said quietly.

The minister pushed through the crowd and, with the stern expression that he wore in the pulpit, halted in front of the enemy soldiers. The townsfolk closed around in a curious ring, and the soldiers were lost to Lemuel's view.

His mother hurried over and grasped his arm, pulling him to his feet. "Did they hurt you?" she asked, trying to brush the mud off his breeches.

"I'm fine," he growled, yanking his arm away.

"Come away home, dear," said his mother. "There's nothing more to do here. It's all over now."

Lemuel looked out across the bay. There in the distance, the British frigate still floated. He remembered the long row of cannon mouths sliding past him in the fog and the gleaming muskets of the Royal Marines.

The eastern sky was lit with a red glow from the burning fort, and the fresh morning breeze bore the smell of smoke. Specks of ash floated from the sky like dark snowflakes.

"All over? No, Ma, I don't think so," he said. "It isn't nearly over yet." The invasion of Sandy Bay was just beginning.

CHAPTER 6

Mrs. Brooks shooed Lemuel along the road to the tavern, occasionally flapping the long skirt of her nightdress at him as though he were a stray chicken. "Get along, now, do," she said when he craned his neck to look back at the beach from whence voices were raised in argument.

"But I have to—"

"No 'buts,'" she said firmly, marching him along the rocky path. "There's work to do. I want you to scrub the taproom floor and polish all the mugs."

"But this is war!" he wailed. "No one scrubs floors in the middle of an invasion!"

"Well, you'll be the first, then," she said. "I know what those fine gentlemen are like, Mr. Pool and the captain and all. They'll want to come down to the tavern, and discuss things over a mug of ale, and tell each other how brave they've been, and plan what to do next." She ran her hands through her hair, disarranging her nightcap. "Oh, dear, they'll be wanting breakfast, like enough, and there's nothing in the house but chowder."

"Make them some gruel," Lemuel muttered crossly. Gruel was his usual breakfast fare on the few mornings when chowder wasn't served.

His mother rapped her knuckles on the top of his head. "Don't give me any of your sauce, young man."

"But, Ma, someone's got to do something—tell the army, the navy, someone!"

"That's not your affair," she snapped. "That's for grown men to decide."

They reached a sprawling building of weathered clapboard shingles and small diamond-paned windows set high in the walls. The tavern stood at the base of Bearskin Neck, only a few yards from the water. The salty breeze from the harbor carried the usual smell of fish and made the sign over the door swing with a rusty creak. Mrs. Brooks opened the door and waved Lemuel inside the dim, empty taproom.

During long summer evenings, the taproom was a cozy place, filled with thirsty fishermen telling yarns, poking fun at the politicians, and complaining about the war. Men lit their pipes with coals from the fire as they sipped cider and ale. But now, in the early morning, the wide, low-roofed room was deserted. No sailors leaned on the oakwood counter that stretched from one wall to the other, and the tables and chairs stood empty.

"Do a good job on that floor, now," Mrs. Brooks ordered, and he groaned aloud. The floorboards were tilted and uneven—he knew from experience that if he dropped a marble in the taproom, it wouldn't know which way to roll first. Scrubbing every corner was a back-breaking task. "And as soon as you've finished," she went on relentlessly, "I want you to go and get me some butter and a couple dozen eggs from the Gott farm—the hens aren't laying a thing these days, and there's hardly an egg in the house. Take Molly so you can get back sooner." Molly was the Brooks family's elderly brown mare, who had drawn the plow and pulled the hay wagon on the farm for as long as Lemuel could remember.

"But, Ma," Lemuel began again, then broke off. An idea had come to him; it flickered in his mind like the uncertain glow of a candle as he considered it carefully—a wild idea, so daring it made him gasp. His mother ignored his protest and began to stack pewter mugs on a tray.

He thought for a moment, then said slowly, "You know, Ma, maybe I should go right now to get the ... eggs. The gentlemen will likely be here any minute, and it's a bit of a ride to the Gott place."

"That's true," she said distractedly, patting her hair. She looked down at her patched nightgown. "And me not even dressed yet! I'll run upstairs and change my clothes, and you get on your way. No dawdling, now, and try to make Molly break out of a walk for once."

"Yes 'm," he said promptly.

"Well, get along," she urged. Abandoning the tray of mugs, she hurried up the stairs. "Remember, two dozen eggs—no, three—fresh, mind, and make sure you don't break any. And get Molly to trot right along, she's as slow as molasses in January. Be firm with her, now!"

"Yes 'm," he said again, heading for the door that led through the pantry to the backyard.

"And come right back!" she called from the top of the stairs.

"Yes 'm!" he shouted over his shoulder, already halfway across the tiny yard. He leaped recklessly over the rows of beans and parsnips in his mother's vegetable patch as he raced to the stable.

Molly lived in a small, rickety shed next to the tavern. Lemuel usually sighed every time he entered it, remembering the big barn with a friendly row of cows and piles of golden hay in the loft. But now he didn't pause to lament the vanished farm; he shot in through the low door like a cannonball.

The sleepy horse tossed her head with a protesting snort. Inside the stable, the air was filled with the smell of hay and manure. Lemuel breathed in the familiar aroma as if it were perfume. Molly's stable was the only place in Sandy Bay that didn't smell of fish.

"Come on, Molly," he said, grabbing the cracked old saddle from its hook on the wall. "We've got work to do." He tossed the saddle across her back. Molly looked around as he tightened the girth, and he grinned at her fiercely. "And I don't mean scrubbing the floor!"

Lemuel saddled and bridled the horse at record speed, then led her out of the stable. He knew that time was precious and that he must ride faster than he ever had before. Swinging himself into the saddle, he clapped his heels into Molly's sides. "Forward!" he shouted.

But Molly was never in a hurry. She lowered her head to snatch a bite of grass.

Lemuel hauled on the reins. "Come on, girl, it's all up to us," he pleaded. "We'll show them who's a traitor." He poked her plump sides with his heels again, and Molly grunted sleepily and started off at her usual plod.

Lemuel shook the reins briskly, urging her out of the yard and across the square. The Sandy Bay townsfolk were still clustered on the beach, surrounding the huddle of red coats; no one noticed him as he steered Molly up the hill, past Mr. Pool's house, toward the Gloucester road.

The road from Sandy Bay to the busy port town of Gloucester was a good one, wide enough for a team of horses. It was mostly used by the stagecoach, which made a round trip each day, except for Sundays. The road took two hours to travel in the lurching, rattling stagecoach; on foot, a brisk walker could make the journey in half that time. And a man galloping on horseback at top speed could get from Sandy Bay to Gloucester in a matter of minutes.

Lemuel had every intention of galloping at top speed. "Come on, Molly, get up!" he cried, flapping the reins about her neck. Molly had never galloped in her life, however, and apparently had no intention of starting now. "Ma's right," said Lemuel in disgust. "You're as slow as molasses." He clapped his heels into her sides again, but she merely snorted ominously and continued her steady gait.

Lemuel jumped off her back. Molly ignored him and kept on going. He broke a long branch from a bush by the side of the road. Scrambling back into the saddle, he raised the stick high. "I'm warning you," he said.

The mare clopped along, then paused to grab a mouthful of grass. "I mean it," he threatened, brandishing the stick near her nose so she could see it. "Ma said to be firm." The mare plodded on, chewing. A long beard of grass dangled from her mouth.

She slowed down even more as she began the steep climb up the church road. Lemuel took a deep breath and leaned back in the saddle. He hated to do it, but this was life and death. "Benedict Arnold," he muttered. "I'll show them." Hardening his heart, he gave her broad backside a gentle smack with the stick.

Such a thing had never happened to the plump old mare before. She tossed up her head in astonishment and bounded off, nearly leaving him behind. Her hooves thundered as she charged up the steep road. They sped away from the ocean and into the wooded center of Cape Ann.

Tall oaks lined the road, their branches arching overhead to make a shadowy green tunnel. The way was straight at first, then the road curved to avoid the marshy lowlands. After a few minutes, Molly slowed her pace while Lemuel gingerly righted himself in the saddle, feeling as though she had jarred loose every one of his teeth. When he glanced over his shoulder, though, he was delighted to see that the road behind was empty. He was first with the news, for sure.

"Caleb Tarr would fall off as soon as you broke into a trot," he told Molly, patting her soft neck. "We'll see who's a turncoat."

By dint of threatening gestures with the stick, he kept Molly moving briskly, and soon her hooves were rattling over the cobbled streets of Gloucester. She slowed down in the tangle of winding lanes and byways near the waterfront, where the streets were empty of all but a few early peddlers. Lemuel looked at the tall shuttered houses, wondering who should hear the great news first, and decided to go straight to the top. Ignoring curious eyes, he inquired the way to the house of Colonel James Appleton, commander of the Gloucester militia.

He reached Colonel Appleton's house, a tall white-fronted home on Prospect Square. The square was empty, the shutters of the big house closed tight. Lemuel flung himself off Molly's back, ran up the steps, and grasped the big iron knocker. He pounded on the door till his hand ached.

After a minute of steady hammering, shutters banged open above him. A nightcapped man thrust his head out of a second-story window. "What's amiss?" shouted a strong voice.

Lemuel took a deep breath. He couldn't quite repress a grin as his shout rose over the sleeping square, waking the echoes with the famous words: "The British are coming!"

The window slammed down immediately. Before Lemuel had time to shout again, the door flew open and a wide-eyed servant ushered him into a dim hall. Lemuel had no time to admire the crystal and china on the mantelpiece and the gold chandelier over his head before a grim-faced Colonel Appleton, clad in dressing gown, nightcap, and slippers, came thundering down the stairs.

"What's to do?" the Colonel demanded. "What's all this about the British?" He reached the bottom of the stairs and strode across the room. He was spare and wiry, with long arms and legs, and so tall that Lemuel's head was on a level with the middle button of his dressing gown. "Speak up, lad, are you a half-wit?" Colonel Appleton stared down, pale blue eyes blazing over a high-bridged nose.

"They've landed! They're attacking Sandy Bay!" Lemuel blurted.

"Sandy Bay?" repeated the Colonel, raising his brows. "Why on earth would they bother with Sandy Bay?"

Lemuel drew himself up, insulted. "Well, we do have a fort, you know," he protested.

Appleton ignored this and pursed his lips, considering. "They must be trying to capture fishing craft, I suppose. What force, how many ships?"

Lemuel took a deep breath and started talking. "Frigate ... cannons ... alarm bell ... fort on fire ..."

Long before he had finished, Appleton ordered, "Wait here!" and bounded back up the stairs.

Used to the pace of Sandy Bay, the boy was astonished at the effect his warning had produced. Colonel Appleton aroused his blinking, yawning servants and sent them speeding from house to house to spread the word for the militia to assemble. He was back downstairs in uniform, every button done up, in less time than it would have taken a Sandy Bay fisherman to bait a hook.

The Colonel strode out the front door, buckling on his sword belt. Lemuel trotted at his heels but stopped short on the doorstep, drawing in his breath in amazement. The cobblestone square was packed with militiamen.

Remnants of the night fog drifted around their knees as they lined up in silent rows. More armed men arrived every minute; hundreds of them filled the broad square and choked the streets. Lemuel watched open-mouthed as the men shouldered their muskets. The cheerful morning sunlight made the polished bayonets glitter.

Colonel Appleton banged the door shut behind him as a servant led a tall white horse up to the doorstep. "All right, boy," said the Colonel. "Lead the way." He swung himself into the saddle, and scowled down at Lemuel.

"L-lead the way?" stammered the boy.

The Colonel looked down his hawk nose. "You do know the way, don't you?"

"Yes, sir!" Lemuel exclaimed, saluting smartly. He climbed aboard Molly and clapped his heels into her sides. The soldiers swung into line behind him.

Lemuel shook his head, hardly able to believe what was happening. His chest swelling with pride, he gleefully imagined his mother watching him lead the troops to the scene of the British invasion. And Bill Tarr and Caleb and all the smug fisher-boys of Sandy Bay—they'd be sorry now! They would stand by the side of the road and gape at him with envy as he rode next to Colonel Appleton at the head of a thousand men.

CHAPTER 7

Colonel Appleton reined in his horse when they reached the silent church on top of the hill. He raised his hand, and the column came to a halt with a stamping of booted feet and a rolling of drums. The Colonel's powerful horse sidled restlessly, and shards of wood from the damaged church tower crunched under his hooves. Lemuel had no need to rein in Molly, who immediately lowered her head and began to nibble at the sparse grass in the churchyard.

There was no sight or sound of the British invaders: no cannon fire, no landing craft, no Redcoats with torches burning the town. The frigate was still clearly visible, however, and Lemuel pointed it out eagerly; it floated at anchor, still far out in the bay, the Union Jack fluttering from the bare mast.

The folk of Sandy Bay were gathered in clusters on the beach and in Dock Square. Children played tag between chatting groups of adults, and laughter rang in the pleasant morning air. Chickens and geese meandered through the gardens that ringed the cottages, and a small pig nosed in the road.

Appleton gave a curt order over his shoulder. The trumpeter blew a deafening blast, and the cheerful noise of talk and laughter faded as the Sandy Bay folk turned to confront the newcomers. Men swung muskets to their shoulders; women grabbed their children.

Colonel Appleton gave another brisk command, and the drums growled like distant thunder. The column began to move ponderously down the road, picking up speed. Lemuel twisted in the saddle to admire the long files of gleaming bayonets. Chickens fled squawking out of the way as the stream of militiamen swept down the hill.

The folk of Sandy Bay lowered their muskets and began to look at each other doubtfully, scratching their heads. Children scurried from the roadway as the marching men stamped by. Sure enough, Caleb and the other boys stood open-mouthed as Lemuel rode past with his nose in the air.

Colonel Appleton shouted orders to the officers riding behind him. They drew their swords, pointing with the shining blades to direct the troops. Some of the soldiers trotted down side streets at the quickstep. Another group raced for the harbor. The Colonel, followed by Lemuel and a large detachment of militiamen, headed straight for Dock Square.

The square was crowded with Sandy Bay folk, who parted reluctantly to let the Colonel's big horse through. Lemuel climbed down from the saddle at the edge of the square and held Molly's rein, awaiting developments. He was a little chilled by the cold glances his neighbors cast at the Colonel and his troops.

Mr. Pool, the Reverend, and a circle of other men were gathered near the big wooden pump. Appleton dismounted, glaring around at the ring of villagers who regarded him with suspicious faces.

"Well, report, someone!" snapped the Colonel. "What's toward? How big is the landing force?"

Captain Benjamin Haskell, commander of the Sea Fencibles, stepped forward, hat in hand. He was a fisherman, a popular young man with a cheerful face, who had just been elected captain. He hadn't had time to put on his uniform and wore only an old pair of trousers pulled over his nightshirt. "We've captured eight men and an officer who were in a landing barge, sir," he said, saluting briskly.

Appleton nodded. "How many casualties?"

"No one was hurt," said Ebenezer Pool, joining them. Colonel Appleton looked him up and down, eyebrows raised high on his narrow forehead. Lemuel grinned. Mr. Pool was still clad in his purple dressing gown.

The Reverend Jewett stepped forward as well. "All are unharmed, thanks to God's grace," he said.

Appleton ignored him. "What's this taradiddle the boy's been telling me about the British sinking their own boat?" he demanded. "Is he crazy?"

"Sunk themselves, by God," said Haskell, grinning. "Flat calm, in the harbor, and she went straight to the bottom. Never seen anything like it."

"That cannon's ours now," added Ebenezer with visible pride. "A prize of war. You know, we should haul it up and do something with it."

"We should put her in the town square!" said Tom Wheeler. "Fire her off on the Fourth of July!" He chuckled, his broad shoulders shaking.

"Put it in the churchyard," suggested the Reverend, rubbing his long chin thoughtfully. "That seems fitting."

"That'll teach 'em!" added Tom. Lemuel joined in the general roar of laughter.

Appleton's sharp voice cut into their mirth. "And where are the prisoners being held?" he demanded.

"Don't worry," said Ebenezer, still chuckling. "We have them safely stowed."

"How many guards are posted?" Appleton looked down his thin nose.

An uneasy silence fell. Ebenezer cleared his throat. Captain Haskell tried to tuck in the tail of his nightshirt. "Well, a few of the lads went along—," Haskell began.

"A few of the lads!" the Colonel exclaimed. "There should be at least a dozen men guarding the enemy at all times." He glared around at the group. "And where are the Sea Fencibles who were stationed at the fort?" he demanded. "There should have been nine of them on duty last night. Why have they not reported?"

There was another echoing silence. Lemuel looked around in surprise. Everyone else looked around as well. No one had noticed, in the confusion, the total absence of the Bearskin Neck garrison. All eyes turned in the direction of the fort at the end of the long peninsula, where a spire of black smoke still rose.

Without a word Colonel Appleton spun around and made for the fort. Most of the Sandy Bay folk followed, as well as some of the Gloucester men. Lemuel tied Molly to a gatepost and elbowed his way in among the crowd.

The mob hastened along the dirt track that led to the tip of Bearskin Neck, the brawny militiamen shoving Lemuel aside. The sheds and cottages that lined the road were empty; the only sign of life was a scrawny cow behind a bait shack, browsing on a pile of fish heads. Gulls wailed overhead.

The odor of smoke grew strong at the end of the Neck, where the ruins of the watchtower still smoldered. The fort was deserted. No sentries stood on the big granite boulders, no guards patrolled outside, no cannons poked their grim black muzzles over the walls. There was no trace of the nine Sea Fencibles.

The crowd of townsfolk and militiamen stared at the charred ruins of the watchtower. Lemuel clambered up on the slippery rocks that lined the water's edge and looked down into the clear depths with a dismal suspicion of what he would see. Sure enough, the dark shapes of the fort's only two cannons lay on the sea bottom where the British soldiers had thrown them. Little silver fish nibbled at the metal and swam in and out of the muzzles.

The graceful British ship in the bay was outlined sharply in the clear morning light. Appleton swung a brass telescope to his eye and frowned across the water. "The *Nymph*," he announced into the silence. "Frigate—thirty-eight guns." No one replied.

"That's it, then," Appleton went on calmly. "It's as plain as a pikestaff what happened. The second enemy barge must have landed here. While you were fishing soldiers out of the other side of the bay, the others got ashore here, heaved the cannons into the water, and burned the fort. No bodies, though, I see— they must have captured the entire garrison of Sea Fencibles." He closed the telescope with a vicious snap. "Not that *that* was much of a feat," he added.

The facts were beginning to sink in. A murmur arose as new-comers hastening down the Neck were told of the missing men. A woman holding a shawl-wrapped baby broke out in a sobbing wail. The noise grew as voices were raised in shouts and curses.

"Come, come," said the Colonel. "No good crying over spilt milk. At least they didn't damage any fishing craft."

Captain Haskell, standing at the Colonel's elbow, cleared his throat and spoke up. "I'll see to getting a boat, sir. You'll be wanting to row out to the frigate."

Appleton raised his brows. "Row to the enemy vessel? To what end, pray?"

"Well, shouldn't we try to arrange the exchange of prisoners as soon as possible?" asked Haskell, surprise on his pleasant round face. "I mean, since we have nine of their men, and they have nine of ours, we'll surely ..."

Lemuel looked eagerly at Appleton, but the Colonel wore a stony expression. "Nonsense!" he said.

Haskell and Mr. Pool exchanged startled glances. "But ... but, sir ...," the Captain stammered.

"Any immediate exchange is out of the question. We must refer the matter to higher authority." The Colonel turned on his heel as Captain Haskell opened his mouth again.

Ebenezer Pool stepped forward with a dignity that was marred by the fact that he was still wearing his long tasseled nightcap. "Come now, Colonel," he said in a reasonable tone. "If the prisoners are taken to England, they'll be imprisoned for the length of the war. Why, we might never see them again."

The Colonel shrugged.

Ebenezer tried once more, gathering his purple robe about him in a dignified manner. "But, surely, sir ... the war could drag on for years ... you know what conditions are like in English prisons." Ebenezer Pool was not a short man, but he had to look up to address the Colonel, as Lemuel did when he argued with his mother.

Haskell stepped forward again, twisting his wool cap between his hands. "I implore you, sir!" His voice rose a notch. "Conditions for prisoners of war are well known to be appalling—they'll be thrown in irons—starve—die of disease. The chances of them ever getting home are—"

Appleton interrupted with a raised forefinger. "I can only repeat my position. All prisoners of war must be turned over to the proper authorities, the Committee of Safety at Salem. I shall immediately send a dispatch informing them of the situation. Any question of exchange will be theirs to consider, but I hardly think it's likely. And that, my good man, is an end to the matter."

The Reverend Jewett cleared his throat and approached with the measured tread he used when mounting the pulpit to begin one of his two-hour sermons. Ebenezer Pool and Captain Haskell at once gave way to him. "Sir," the Reverend began in his deep voice. "It is clear to me that—"

"I don't give a damn what is, or is not, clear to you, sir!"

the Colonel interrupted him. Contradicting the Reverend was unheard of in Sandy Bay, and Lemuel gasped. The Colonel was as tall as the minister; they stood a few inches apart, almost nose to nose. "A parson has no jurisdiction whatsoever in this matter," the Colonel went on in icy tones. He turned to Haskell and Ebenezer Pool, who stood openmouthed. "Gloucester is the main township, of which Sandy Bay is merely a parish. I, and I alone, have the final say in this matter." He raised his narrow eyebrows. "You may be leading citizens here, but you are, so to speak, only big fish in a very small pond."

Appleton swept away, trailed by his blue-uniformed officers. The Sandy Bay folk watched him march off as black smoke from the ruined fort wreathed around them.

Ebenezer Pool's face was scarlet. "God's holy trousers!" he burst out.

Lemuel's eyes widened, and he eyed the Reverend, but the minister ignored the blasphemy; he stood quietly with his back to the crowd and gazed out at the ship, rubbing his chin.

"Small pond be damned!" Ebenezer Pool sputtered. "Well, that's a Gloucesterman for you. Cursed fellow's like talking to a brick wall. We could have had a more reasonable conversation with a halibut."

Captain Haskell sank down on an upturned dory, running a hand through his lank hair as he looked at the charred remnants of the watchtower. "What in God's name are we going to do, Eb?" he asked. Lemuel listened eagerly, sure Mr. Pool would have the solution, and was appalled when his wealthy neighbor shrugged.

"I don't know, Ben." Ebenezer sighed, then pulled off his nightcap and stuffed it in a pocket. "I don't know."

"You think if we contacted the Committee of Safety—"

"The committee," said Ebenezer scornfully. "By the time they entertain debate, consider the options, and propose a motion, the boys'll have been in prison for a year."

"But if we told them it was an emergency—"

"You've been to meetings of the committee, Ben," said Ebenezer.

"Well, yes," Ben admitted, nodding sadly. "Well, then, *you* think of something, Eb. You know that no one the British get their hands on ever comes home again." He jerked his head toward the weeping woman who clutched the baby to her breast. "Amos Storey was in the fort, and Mary's just had her first. And Johnny Rowe's gone, too."

A bearded fisherman joined in. "My Sarah's two brothers are taken. What'll I tell her?"

"Isaac Dade, and Abner Tarr, John Norwood, and the Babson cousins," added Tom Wheeler, counting the tale of nine on his fingers. "Not a family in Sandy Bay that isn't related to one of those lads."

A woman stood by the ruined watchtower, staring out to sea, dry-eyed. Her white hair streamed back from her face in the salty wind. Lemuel knew she was Abner Tarr's mother. Amos Storey's wife and the other womenfolk of the captured garrison gathered beside her on the rocks, gazing at the warship on the wide, sunlit bay.

Lemuel looked from the ruined fort to the water, as though

hoping to spot some trace of the vanished men. The only movement from the frigate was the red and blue flag fluttering from the mainmast. There was no sign of a battle; no blood; no bodies; nothing. He had never imagined a story with an ending like this.

Tom Wheeler and a few of the other fishermen began to dump buckets of seawater on the smoldering boards of the watchtower. "Come on, boy, don't stand about when there's work to be done!" Bill Tarr handed Lemuel a bucket. "Bear a hand."

Lemuel filled a wooden bucket with seawater and lugged it to the ruins. He splashed the clear water over a heap of charred wood that still glowed orange at the edges. There was a loud hiss, and he stepped back, coughing as the steam and ashes stung his throat and filled his eyes with tears. The sour, fishy, burnt odor was the bitter smell of defeat.

CHAPTER 8

The smoldering watchtower was finally quenched, and the crowd began to disperse. Tom Wheeler tossed his bucket down with a sigh. "Would have done better to build that lighthouse after all," he remarked to Bill Tarr, pulling at his long beard. "Reverend told us so, often enough." Bill just snorted as he shuffled away.

Tom glanced Lemuel's way, looking him up and down with raised eyebrows. "You're the new boy at the tavern, aren't you?"

Lemuel nodded, a little shy of the big man. "We just moved here."

"Not from Gloucester, are you?" Tom inquired suspiciously.

"No, we had a farm at Pride's Crossing."

"Ah," Tom said. "Inland." He pursed his lips. "Well, at least you're not a Gloucesterman." The fisherman nodded and headed down the path back toward the village center. Lemuel followed, wondering if his new neighbor had any idea what to do about the British. He had to stretch his legs to keep up with Tom's long strides.

They walked down the length of Bearskin Neck, passing bait shacks and cottages that lined the rutted, pot-holed road. Lemuel wrinkled his nose as they went by rows of drying racks draped with long white strips of cod, like laundry hung on clotheslines.

Tom jammed his hands into his pockets. "Damned meeching colonel," he muttered. "Like to pull that long nose for him." He gave a sigh. "Suppose he has a point about the Sea Fencibles, though," he admitted. "Sandy Bay folk aren't much use at soldiering, really. Can't seem to get the hang of it."

"Well, the war's lasted two years," Lemuel pointed out. "You've had plenty of time to practice."

"Oh no, we're right fresh at the job," said Tom. "Sea Fencibles were just mustered a few months ago. Before that, all Cape Ann fishermen had an exemption—that means the governor let us off the hook—said we was 'mariners' and didn't have to learn the soldiering trade. Then a British frigate sailed by last summer, and everyone got so jumpy that they built the fort. Made us all join up." He shrugged. "Ah, well, the missus says even soldiering's safer than fishing."

They reached the footpath that led to the harbor. "I've got to go make sure *Eliza Jane*'s all right," Tom said. "You'd better get home, boy."

"Is Eliza Jane your missus?" asked Lemuel.

Tom laughed out loud. "My boat," he said. "Ah, she's a sweet little lady, she is. Never been known to nag and don't mind if a hard-working man takes a drop now and again." His grin faded. "She's raring to go, but I can't take her out these days. Not with the blasted Britishers hovering everywhere like sharks around a dead whale." He looked past the harbor, out to sea, and shook his head. "Haven't been out to the banks in six months."

"What are the banks?" Lemuel asked, looking seaward curiously. The blue line of horizon was blank: no land in sight at all. "Are they far out?"

"Far? Why, the Grand Banks are off Canada, of course!" said Tom, staring at him incredulously. "A week's cruise to get there, and cold as a witch's ... why, the cold'll freeze your hands to the lines so you can't let go." He flexed thick fingers that were scribbled over with scars. "But the cod are thick as fleas on a dog's back. As soon as the blasted war is over, I'll be heading out again. That's where the real fishing is."

He nodded to Lemuel and hurried off toward the cluster of masts in the harbor. Lemuel continued on his way to Dock Square, trying to imagine spending an entire week in a boat.

When he reached Molly, she didn't greet him with her usual soft nicker. The mare was plainly still annoyed at so much hurry, and tossed her head when he tried to stroke her. As soon as she was untied, she jerked the reins from his hand and headed back to the stable on her own. He trudged behind her as though his shoes were made of lead. He had never been so tired.

In the stable, Lemuel tugged the heavy saddle off Molly's back, rubbed her down well, and then pitchforked her manger full of the tough salt-marsh hay. The mare sniffed at the pile, then gave a disdainful snort. He threw in a large handful of oats, and she snuffled her nose into the manger, thrusting aside the crackling hay to get at the grain.

"Come on, old girl, don't be mad," he said, patting her smooth neck. "We showed them, you know. We got the minutemen, just like Concord and Lexington." He rubbed the bruise on his chest where Caleb Tarr had shoved him. "I'm as patriotic as the next man. I'm no Benedict Arnold."

Molly didn't raise her head from the oats. She had always been his most sympathetic listener, the only one who never ignored him. Hot tears pricked his eyelids. "All right, give me the cold shoulder," he said in a choked voice. "I guess I deserve it." He left the shed, rubbing his sleeve over his eyes.

He crossed the yard, and as he stepped carefully over the rows of beans in the vegetable patch, he had a distinct feeling that someone was watching him. He glanced over his shoulder, and a sudden movement—a flash of white—made him jump. But he blew out his breath in annoyance when he saw that it was his mother's clothesline, stockings and underlinen and nightshirts billowing in the sea wind. The empty sleeves waved at him mockingly.

He ducked under the flapping laundry and continued across the yard. But the feeling of being watched persisted so strongly that he stopped and spun completely around. "Who's there?" he cried. No one answered.

A blue line of water was visible between the wind-stunted bushes that fenced the yard. There was the frigate, far out on the horizon. He could just make out the gunports, each with a round black muzzle aimed at the town. The British captain was undoubtedly scanning the shore at this very moment; Lemuel almost thought he could catch the glint of the brass telescope. He turned away and hurried across the yard, feeling the captain's pale stare fixed on his back.

Swinging the pantry door open, he entered the dim little

room and slammed the door behind him. The familiar smells of dried apples and pinewood kindling were comforting. He was glad to be safe at home.

A small, shuffling sound caught his ear. He stopped abruptly, glaring around, every muscle tense. Sure enough, there, in the darkest corner, crouched a shadow that began to move.

Lemuel's jaw dropped as the figure straightened above the barrels and stacks of firewood, rising to a towering height. The man came toward him out of the shadows: a burly soldier, clad in the scarlet coat and white crossbelts of His Majesty's Royal Marines.

CHAPTER 9

Lemuel and the enemy soldier stood face-to-face. The Redcoat was holding a bowl in his hand, one of his mother's best pieces of pewter—the second wave of the attack must be underway, and the soldiers were looting! Lemuel looked wildly around for a weapon, grabbed up a garden spade that leaned against the wall, and held it in front of himself like a shield. He was opening his mouth to shout for help when the man stepped forward into a ray of sun from the window. Lemuel recognized the cheerful face and gap-toothed grin of Sergeant Archer.

Then his mother's voice called from the taproom. "What on earth is taking you so long, Sergeant? Have you found the sugar barrel yet? Look sharp!"

"Not yet, ma'am," called the soldier. "It's a bit dark in the corners here." He nodded sociably to Lemuel. "Well, well, nice to run into you again, mate. It's a small world, so it is. Now, tell me, where might the sugar barrel be?"

"What?" said Lemuel, his mind blank with amazement.

"The sugar barrel," the soldier repeated patiently.

"Oh," said Lemuel, lowering the spade. "Um ... over there." He pointed to a small cask in the corner of the pantry.

"Right, thanks," said the soldier with a nod. He dipped the

pewter bowl into the barrel and brought it up filled with sugar. "Better put that shovel down, lad, you'll break something. Here we are, ma'am," he called cheerfully, strolling into the taproom. Lemuel followed but stopped short on the threshold, transfixed by the astonishing sight of his mother surrounded by a crowd of red-coated soldiers.

"About time," she said to the Sergeant, wiping her hands on her apron. She took the bowl and poured some sugar into a small kettle that simmered over the fire. Lemuel knew the spicy fragrance well; it brought back long winter nights in the farm kitchen. "I put in just a touch of nutmeg and a trifle of cinnamon," she said, stirring the pot. "Now if I was to add lemons, this punch would be something special. But they're so hard to come by these days, with the war and all. I'm not wasting my lemons on the likes of you."

"Oh, it'll be a treat, ma'am, never fear," said the tall soldier. "By the bye, would this be the boy you were looking for?"

"Oh, thank heavens, there you are!" His mother rubbed her arm across her forehead, her face red from bending over the fire. "I was just starting to worry. What a time you've been! Honestly, if that horse went any slower she'd be walking backward." She stirred the kettle again. "Turns out I don't need the eggs after all. Mr. Pool sent the prisoners here, and the town will pay for their keep, but I can't afford to waste poached eggs on this lot. Now don't run off—bustle about and get some blankets and a few more mugs." She shot a look at Sergeant Archer out of the corner of her eye. "The punch is almost ready, it's fine and warming. That water in the bay is cold enough to freeze beer." She shook a dishtowel at her son, who still stood rooted to the floor with astonishment. "Bustle about!"

Lemuel bustled; he scurried behind the counter and began to take down chipped clay mugs from a high shelf and stack them on a tray, still only half-able to believe what he was seeing.

One of the soldiers, a straw-haired boy with big hands and awkward feet, sneezed loudly. Mrs. Brooks shook her head and laid her hand on the arm of his coat. "My word, you're still soaked to the bone. Honestly, you've been standing around in those wet clothes half the morning. You'd better get those jackets off."

She hauled a big willow basket out of the pantry and smacked it down on the kitchen floor. "Put your wet things in here, and I'll hang them on the line," she ordered. "That's good wool cloth. I don't want it to shrink—I might be able to get a quilt out of that." The morning sun slanted through the windows and made the scarlet coats glow red as blood. "That's it, look sharp," she said as one of the men handed her a sodden jacket. "Stand on the hearthstone there, and don't go dripping on the rug."

Lemuel handed round the mugs, recognizing one by one the soldiers he had met on the moonlit deck in what seemed like another century.

"My eye, this is the coziest jail I've ever been in," remarked Martin. He was the thin, dark-eyed man with a nose as sharp as a needle. He looked around the taproom, warmed by the fire and lit by the sun that poured in the diamond-paned windows, and the deep lines around his mouth relaxed in a narrow smile.

"You should know jails, Will, you've been in enough of

'em," replied Archer, and his grin reminded Lemuel of Tom Wheeler's. In fact, without their uniforms, the British looked pretty much like any group of Sandy Bay fishermen. His father had once showed him an engraving of a battle scene in which the British soldiers all had neatly curled white hair and pigtails, but these folk had brown or black or yellow hair like anybody else, badly bedraggled from their swim in the bay. Their accent reminded him that they were from another country, though; even the simplest words sounded unfamiliar.

"I thought all Yankees lived in barns." A lanky soldier shivered as he drew closer to the fire.

"Keep a civil tongue in your head, Hill," snapped a young man, his wet, dark hair streaked down the sides of his pale face. His coat had gold loops of braid on the arms, and Lemuel remembered the youthful lieutenant who had been in charge of the landing party. "We're guests of these good people," the officer said sternly.

"Aye, sir," replied Hill. "Should'na look a gift horse in the mouth, they say." He watched Mrs. Brooks as she threw more wood on the fire and stirred the kettle again.

"Get your coat off, too, lad," she said to the young officer. "Wrap up in a blanket before you catch your death."

"Thank you, madam," he replied. He spoke more understandably than the others, though with an elegant accent that was distinctly different from the Massachusetts nasal twang. "This is most kind of you," he added, sweeping a deep bow. "Allow me to present myself. I am Lieutenant Hurley, of His Majesty's Royal Marines, at your service."

"My, nicely spoken, dear," said Mrs. Brooks, patting him on the back. "Now step up to the fire, and take those boots off, too. You've already brought in more mud than a pig."

The soldiers crowded around the hearth, their white shirts and breeches still dripping cold water, as she took a bottle of rum from a shelf behind the counter and carefully poured a large dollop into the pot. The men watched her every movement as she ladled the steaming mixture from the kettle into the mugs, then handed them out. The soldiers nodded their thanks and warmed their hands around the cups of steaming punch. When his mother was busy with the basket heaped with coats, Lemuel helped himself to a ladleful. The fragrant brew burned his tongue and made him choke, but it warmed him down to his cold toes.

"I must again express my gratitude, madam." Lieutenant Hurley looked even younger now that he had shed his gold-laced coat and was wrapped in a patchwork quilt. "We are deeply obliged to you."

"That we are, ma'am," added Martin and drained his cup of punch, his long nose disappearing into the mug as he tilted it back. He drew a deep breath and smacked his lips. "The last thing we expected was to be offered a round of grog," he observed.

"Life's full of pleasant surprises, mate," remarked Archer. He raised his drink in a toast to Mrs. Brooks, and she giggled. Lemuel looked at her in astonishment.

"Life's full of unpleasant surprises, too," Martin pointed out. "We didn't expect to be having a swim in the bay."

Archer took a loud sip of the steaming punch, then lowered his mug abruptly and cocked his head as if listening. Lieutenant Hurley looked up quickly, and then Lemuel heard it, too—the approaching sound of booted marching feet.

Lieutenant Hurley cast off the quilt he was wrapped in and stood up straight as the soldiers looked at each other uneasily. Lemuel held his empty tray tightly and stared at the door. The thud of footsteps drew nearer, then halted at a sharp command. The taproom door was thrust open and hit the wall with a bang, making them all jump. Colonel Appleton stood in the doorway.

"Just as I thought!" he cried. He surveyed the prisoners with narrowed eyes. The British soldiers stood frozen, mugs in their hands. "I want six armed guards in here!" Appleton bellowed over his shoulder. "And a sentry at each door outside. At the double!"

A half-dozen militiamen ran in, each carrying a long musket. Sentries appeared outside the windows. The guards were all Gloucestermen, strangers to Lemuel; they ignored him and his mother as they took up their positions at the doors and windows, wool caps pulled low over their brows. Each man slapped his hands to his sides and stood at rigid attention.

The Colonel glanced down at Lemuel, not seeming to recognize him. "Shut those windows, boy," he ordered. Lemuel didn't budge. One of the officers hurried around the taproom, swinging the shutters tightly closed. The light grew dimmer with each bang.

"Now just a minute, sir!" Mrs. Brooks cried, hands on hips,

her plump face stern. "This is my tavern, I'll have you know. You can't just invade the place like this—"

"My good woman, I most certainly can," said the Colonel over his shoulder. "And I'll have you know there are severe penalties for those who offer aid and comfort to the enemy."

Lemuel stepped forward, opening his mouth angrily, and the Colonel glanced down at him. Appleton's nose lifted as if he detected a bad smell, and the words died on Lemuel's tongue.

The Colonel held out his hand to Mrs. Brooks. "I'll trouble you for the door key." Mrs. Brooks stared at him for a long minute, then lowered her eyes. She slowly unfastened the key from the jingling bunch at her belt.

The Colonel gave a slight bow as she handed it over. "My apologies if we incommode you, madam, it will not be for long," he said, eyeing the silent row before him. "The prisoners will be taken under armed guard to Salem as soon as possible, where they can be properly incarcerated." He looked pointedly at the steaming kettle of sugar and rum. "Until that time," he announced, "the Punch Bowl Tavern is closed."

CHAPTER 10

Lemuel sat in the dark, crouching at the top of the stairs that led from the taproom to the second floor of the tavern, and listened to the loud tick of his father's old clock on the mantel. The clock clanked and whirred and began to strike the hour. He counted the slow strokes, one by one, till he reached twelve.

He yawned; his eyelids were as heavy as if the hour were midnight, but it was only noon. Bright sparks of sun gleamed through the chinks in the shutters. He'd been sitting there for half an hour, but he felt as though several days had passed since the Colonel had stamped out of the taproom with a slam that shook the old tavern to its foundations. Lemuel listened, but all was quiet downstairs. The Colonel was safely gone.

He crept down a few steps and peered into the taproom, his face pressed against the banister rails. The British prisoners were huddled together on the floor or lying on their blankets, staring at the smoke-stained ceiling. Lieutenant Hurley sat with his head in his hands. The Gloucestermen were taking things easier now that the Colonel had gone off to post dispatches; they were lined up at the counter, talking and laughing over mugs of cider.

Lemuel cautiously cleared his throat, and Sergeant Archer,

sitting on the floor in his still-damp red coat, glanced up and caught his eye. They looked at each other through the bars of the railing. Lemuel opened his mouth, then closed it again, unable to think of a thing to say.

"Well, lad," said Archer in a low voice. "I asked you if your folk poured a drop on account. We owe your mother for a very pleasant sup of punch."

The other prisoners were sitting nearby, deep in conversation. Martin looked up and gave Lemuel a brief nod, then returned to his muttered argument with Hill. "And then I *told* you not to put in so much powder, but would you listen? No, not you."

"Lieutenant said to give her a double charge," Hill protested.

"Only a feckless greenhorn like you would do it, though. Don't you have any notion—"

"Silence in the ranks!" ordered Lieutenant Hurley. One of the guards glared across the room, and Lemuel withdrew into the shadows till the sentry looked away and resumed sipping at his mug.

"What do you think's going to happen?" Lemuel whispered to the Sergeant, under cover of a burst of laughter from the jovial Gloucestermen.

Archer gave a ghost of his usual grin. "Who knows? Looks like a long war." He shrugged. "No one at home'll miss me, anyway." The sentries glanced their way again, and one sat up and frowned, reaching for his musket. Lemuel retreated back up the stairs.

He sat on the top step and leaned wearily against the banister. He wished he could do something—anything!—but no matter how he racked his tired brain, he couldn't think of anything useful to do. The ticking of the clock blended with the faint footsteps of the sentries outside the door and the murmur of the prisoners' hopeless voices. The shadows around him blurred together as his eyelids grew heavy. He finally fell asleep sitting up, his cheek resting on the hard wooden rail.

"Stop hanging about with that long face!" Lemuel's mother scolded him as he idled about the kitchen after awakening from his long nap. The kitchen was a cramped, narrow space behind the taproom, hung with strings of onions and dried apples; the little room was uncomfortably hot whenever the cooking fire was burning.

His mother bent over a bubbling kettle of chowder, stirring energetically with a long wooden spoon. Lemuel sniffed the fishy smell and stuck out his tongue behind his mother's back. Chowder was the staple food of Sandy Bay, and his mother always had a kettle of it simmering over the fire: haddock chowder, cod chowder, mackerel chowder—whatever bits were too small to go on the drying racks were sold cheap for the pot. He couldn't restrain a sigh.

"And stop sighing like that, or you'll blow me away," his mother added. "There's work to be done."

"I scrubbed the counter twice," he protested. "And I carried water and filled the wood box. I can't scrub the floor, there's people lying on it. Now there's nothing to do."

"If you have so much free time on your hands, then you'll just have to go to school," she said. "The Reverend's been after me to send you for a week now."

"I don't need to go to school!" Lemuel hated the very thought of the long, strict hours on a bench that was even more uncomfortable than a church pew. "I can read already! It's nothing but girls and babies at this school, anyway, the boys go out fishing as soon as they turn seven. Besides, I have too much work to do."

"Well, go and do it, then!" she snapped. "Or it's off to school with you."

Lemuel scrubbed the dark wood of the taproom counter for the third time, rubbing listlessly at the scars left by countless mugs of beer and cider. He tried to catch Sergeant Archer's eye again, but the guards were now sitting around the fire only a few feet away, and the prisoners were all asleep or staring at the floor.

After a midday dinner of halibut chowder, Mrs. Brooks told Lemuel to run down to the harbor. "See if they have any fish heads to spare," she ordered. "I need something to put in the chowder pot."

He looked up, his eyes brightening. For once he didn't object to an errand at the harbor. "Yes 'm," he said promptly and raced out the kitchen door before she could change her mind.

He ran through the taproom, flung open the front door, and darted between the two sentries that stood at rigid attention just outside. One of the guards, a lean Gloucester fisherman with a drooping mustache, raised his musket. "Get back here, boy," he commanded. "What are you about?"

"Ah, leave him," said the other sentry, yawning. "He's too small to bother with." Lemuel scooted around the corner before they could finish the argument.

He reveled in the release from the endless round of chores in the stuffy, shuttered tavern and breathed in the salty wind gratefully. The night's fog had vanished, and the air was as clear and sharp as cider. Bright goldenrod poked from every crack in the red rocks that lined the water, and the elms had a touch of gold in their rustling leaves. He was in no hurry to return to work in the hot kitchen, and before going to the harbor he made a detour to see if anything interesting was afoot in Dock Square.

He stopped, dismayed, as soon as he turned the corner. A boisterous crowd of Gloucestermen had displaced the usual cluster of chatting fishermen's wives, and no children were in sight, bowling hoops or playing tag. Soldiers lounged about the pump, roughhousing and laughing. A group of militiamen had set up a target and were holding a noisy musket practice in the flat stretch behind the blacksmith shop that was the Sea Fencibles' drill yard. Armed sentries stood everywhere, posted in the streets and all along the shore road that skirted the bay. Lemuel hastily turned around and went back down Bearskin Neck.

The Neck was almost deserted. Only a few fishermen were about, mending nets or using short, blunt knives to open clams for bait. He didn't know any of the men by name and felt shy about asking strangers for news. Just past the tavern, he turned off the main track that led to the fort and trotted down the footpath to the harbor.

The little harbor was a natural inlet in the rocky wall of the Neck, a round basin of water, calm but deep. Its arms of granite cradled Sandy Bay's fishing boats, sheltering them from storm winds. Lemuel stood on one of the high stone piers that fringed the harbor and looked around for a familiar face.

Across the harbor, he spotted Reverend Jewett, leaning down from the dock to talk with Bill Tarr. The old fisherman stood upright in his bobbing boat, a hand cupped around his ear to catch the minister's words. Bill had been pitchforking the heavy fish from last night's catch up onto the dock, but the fish lay forgotten as the two men talked.

The Reverend bent closer toward the dory as the breeze fluttered the tails of his long frock coat. Bill put down the pitchfork, looked around cautiously, and climbed up onto the dock to continue the low-voiced conversation. The minister put a hand on his shoulder, and they leaned their heads together intently.

The Reverend noticed Lemuel loitering and waved him away with an imperious hand. "Get about your business, boy."

Lemuel scurried away, studying the pair curiously over his shoulder. Bill never went near the church and often sat in the tavern complaining how the minister was after him again to give up drinking on Sundays. What could he and the Reverend be talking about in such a friendly manner? Lemuel shrugged, too accustomed to the secrecy of adults to puzzle over it for long.

Wondering what was afoot on the British ship, he glanced across the harbor, out to sea. Without thinking about it, he was starting to develop the fisherman's habit of always noting the tide level. The water was low now, and brown strands of seaweed were draped over the rocks along the shore. Cormorants fished lazily, poking their beaks into the clear water. Beyond Bearskin Neck, the ocean spread out like a wide blue carpet, with ripples of white lace where the water met the shore. He noticed that the frigate had moved further away, closer to the northern tip of Cape Ann, by Halibut Point.

"Think the Limeys are up to anything?" a voice called unexpectedly below him. Startled, Lemuel looked down. Tom Wheeler sat in a wide, blunt-nosed craft that bobbed at anchor in the low water near the pier. He was repairing a thick strand of rope, his big hands deftly weaving the frayed cords together.

Lemuel shrugged in answer to the question and sat down on the pier, his dangling feet on a level with Tom's head. "How's *Eliza Jane?*" he inquired, admiring the boat; she was a good-size sailing vessel, painted a cheerful yellow, with her name in blue letters on her side.

"She seems all right." Tom stroked the smooth yellow planking. "Lucky for those Lobsterbacks she is," he added darkly. "If they laid a finger on her, they'd be sorry." He spat over the side.

"That ship's awful quiet out there," said Lemuel. "What'll we do if they come—"

"You there! Wheeler!" A deep voice interrupted him. Reverend Jewett was approaching, with Bill Tarr at his heels. The minister waved a hand at Tom. "A word, if you please."

"Certainly!" Tom shouted back. "What can I do for you, Reverend?"

The Reverend frowned, glancing from side to side. "Over here," he said in a low voice. He placed a finger across his lips and beckoned.

Tom raised thick brows. He clambered up the ladder to the pier, where he and the minister talked in hushed voices. Lemuel strained his ears to hear as the two men whispered with their heads together.

A hand pinched his shoulder. "Ah, there you are, boy, idling again!" Bill Tarr stood just behind him. He had found a new pipe to replace the one he had lost last night, and a spiral of gray smoke curled about his head. "Take a step along this way," he invited, giving Lemuel a shove. "I've got just the job for you, mate. After all, you wanted to learn the fishing trade, and we never got a chance to finish up last night."

Tom looked over from his conversation with Reverend Jewett and nodded approvingly. "That's it," he called. "Teach him the craft."

"Come along, boy," said Bill. "I'll learn you something every fisherman needs to know."

"What's that?" asked Lemuel suspiciously.

Bill smiled and patted him on the back. "How to clean fish."

<hr/>

The slow afternoon wore on; it seemed an age till the sun disappeared below a seashell-pink horizon. A breeze kicked up whitecaps on the bay as evening fell, and the night mist began to rise from the water. Lemuel finally escaped from Bill Tarr's watchful eye and the gory pile of codfish. He trudged back to the tavern, carrying a heavy bucket of bloody fish heads.

His mother threw up her hands and wrinkled her nose at his smell. She made him scrub all over and change his shirt before he sat down to supper. But no matter how much soap he used, his palms still smelled of fish.

Mrs. Brooks carried a kettle of chowder into the taproom for the prisoners and the guards. She returned to the kitchen, setting two brimming bowls for herself and Lemuel on the tiny table in front of the fireplace.

"Chowder again," he muttered.

"Be grateful for your food." His mother took off her apron with a weary sigh and sat down across from him.

"We have chowder for every meal, even breakfast," he said. "*And* dinner."

"Don't give me your sauce, young man. Anyway, it's something different tonight—haddock chowder."

He made a face at the bowl of thick gray soup as he picked up his spoon reluctantly.

As they ate, the sea mist began to curl about the tavern, and a woolly whiteness pressed against the windows like a blanket draped over the house. The blank windowpanes made Lemuel feel uncomfortably shut in. He had grown used to being able to see for miles, gazing out across the ocean through the wavy glass of the tavern windows, and he liked watching the boats going to and fro across the bay. The fog made the small kitchen seem even smaller.

At bedtime he trudged up the stairs. The candle he carried pushed the shadows aside, giving a cheerful glow to the dark walls. Halfway up the steps he turned to look down at the taproom, where the prisoners were rolled in blankets on the hearth or curled up on the floor under the tables. The militiamen who guarded them sat comfortably with their boots propped on the counter, instead of standing at attention. Two of them were bent over an absorbing game of checkers. Lemuel went slowly up the stairs, feet dragging, to his tiny room under the eaves.

He set his candle on the bedside table and looked out the low window. There was nothing to see but fog and the reflection of the candle in the glass panes. His mother popped her head in at his door. "Don't open the window, dear, the night air's so bad for the lungs," she said. "Get to bed, now."

"'Night," he said absently, still trying to see out the window. He got into his nightshirt, then climbed into bed and lay on his back, gazing up at the low, slanting ceiling.

The candle lit the room with a faint glow, and in a corner he could see a cobweb that had somehow escaped his mother's vigilance. He lay staring up at the shadowy web. As he had done every night since he'd left the farm, he thought of the comfortable farmhouse and the warm smell of hay in the barn full of hens and cows. He listened in vain for the sweet music of crickets chirping in the hayfields, but the only sounds he could hear were the endless drone of the waves on the rocks and the occasional wail of a gull.

He was uneasily aware of the frigate still in the bay—hovering like a shark, as Tom had said—and of the wide sea that stretched out beyond the land. He could feel the ocean's vast invisible presence under the fog, as though the town stood at the edge of an unseen cliff.

He blew out the candle. *Everything's all right,* he thought, burrowing his head into the pillow. There was no reason to be afraid. Colonel Appleton was in charge, and the danger to Sandy Bay was past. Everything was secure, sentries were posted, and the British invaders were safely under lock and key. All was well, and he ought to be cheerful and, indeed, thoroughly pleased with himself. He just couldn't figure out why he felt so much like crying.

CHAPTER 11

Lemuel woke from a dream, his heart pounding, and sat straight up in bed. For an instant he was still in the boat, lost on a dark sea and surrounded by sea monsters with long necks that turned into the masts of warships. He stared into the darkness, expecting to feel the tossing of Bill's dory, but the mattress beneath him was as steady as usual. The room was quiet, faintly lit by the moonlight that stole through the small window.

He sat blinking for a minute, then lay down and pulled the blanket over his head and tried to get back to sleep. But his eyes wouldn't stay shut, no matter how often he closed them. He turned over and sighed, and turned again, the straw mattress crackling and crunching as he flopped.

Finally, he kicked off the quilt that had tangled around his legs. He got up and went to the window that was a rectangle of pale light under the sloping roof of his small room. The fog had blown out to sea, and the milky shine of moonlight filled the sky and washed away the stars; it was brighter outside than in the house. On the crest of the hill, the damaged tower of the Old Sloop church shone ghostly white. He swung the window open to let the cool night air flow in.

Just below the window, he heard a quiet cough. He leaned out and could see the round woolen caps of the Gloucester guardsmen directly beneath him; three of the sentries leaned against the wall by the tavern door, chatting in low tones.

Lemuel leaned his elbows on the sill, drowsy. Old elm trees overhung the path in front of the tavern, and the rustling of their leaves blended sleepily with the sound of the ocean. He yawned and felt his eyelids closing.

Then he sat up straight, frowning. A shadow had moved under the elms. Staring into the darkness till his eyes ached, he searched the night for a hint of a red coat or the gleam of a musket. His ears strained for the thump of marching feet, but there was only the steady hum of the waves beating on Bearskin Neck. He caught the movement again—an indistinct shape that slid from one patch of darkness to another. *That couldn't be the British*, he thought. The white crossbelts of the Royal Marines would show up at night like a flag.

He watched intently for a while, but nothing else stirred. The movement must have been just the wind blowing the low-drooping branches of the elms. He yawned and decided to go back to bed.

The salt breeze smelled good, but he remembered his mother's warning about the unhealthy night air. He was about to swing the casement shut when he caught sight of someone trotting quickly across the square.

Sandy Bay folk often were out and about at odd hours, but this was no casual fisherman off on a late cruise—the man was moving in a rapid, purposeful crouch, silently, like a raccoon approaching a chicken coop. As the figure moved into a patch of moonlight, Lemuel gasped: the man's face was blackened, with streaks of red war paint across his forehead. Another person moved out from under the trees to join the first, then they both hastily ducked into the shadows.

Bewildered, Lemuel drew in his breath to shout a warning to the guards lounging below him. Then he caught sight of another figure. This one was making no attempt at concealment, striding confidently along the road from the church—a tall man, walking with a swift stride as the skirts of his black coat fluttered behind him.

Lemuel stared. Then, slowly, a smile began to spread across his face. He looked down at the chatting guards again and grinned.

He closed the window silently and tiptoed down the narrow hall, past the open door of the bedroom where his mother slept. He crept down the stairs, careful not to let them creak, and peeked into the taproom.

All was quiet. The room was lit with a warm glow from the embers of the fire. The Royal Marines were still huddled in quilts and blankets, sleeping soundly on the floor. The Gloucester militiamen dozed or played checkers by the light of a lone candle. The only sound was the clock ticking on the mantel and faint snores. Lemuel waited, crouched on the broad landing.

There came a rustle, and then a distinct scuffling sound, just outside the taproom door. The guards continued their checker game undisturbed. A sudden cry was cut off short; the guards jerked up their heads, but before they could reach for their muskets the door banged wide open. A blast of cold wind blew out the candle.

A tide of men flooded into the room, a dozen terrifying scarecrows with faces painted black and red, wearing rags and tatters, and hats pulled low over their eyes. They charged in eerie silence, spreading out across the room in a purposeful rush. The Gloucester militiamen were rolled out of their chairs before they had time to shout. Each guard struggled to free himself, but three or four men gathered around each of the sentries, deftly tying their hands and feet and stuffing gags in their mouths. The British prisoners struggled to their feet, unwinding quilts from around their legs and stumbling over stools and chairs in the dimly-lit room.

"It's a lot of bleedin' savages!" exclaimed Martin, staring at the intruders' painted hands and faces.

"Shut up!" ordered one of the strangers, a broad-chested man with a black beard fringing the bottom of his red-painted face. Lemuel, standing on the stairs watching with glee, immediately recognized Tom Wheeler.

At the base of the staircase, a stout man was sitting on a struggling Gloucesterman, trying to shove a rolled-up kerchief between his clenched teeth. "Hold still, blast your eyes," he muttered to his flailing captive. Ebenezer Pool's red hair peeped from underneath the ragged wool cap. The Gloucesterman, a burly fellow, managed to free an arm. Tipping Ebenezer off him with a crash, the man opened his mouth to bellow for help.

Lemuel, desperate to silence the man, launched himself in

a wild leap from the stairs. By good luck he crashed facedown on the man's head and shoulders, which effectively cut off his shout. The Gloucesterman thrashed fiercely, bouncing Lemuel onto the floor, but Ebenezer Pool and two other men fell on top of the captive and trussed him up in short order.

"Thankee, lad," Mr. Pool muttered, nodding to Lemuel, who nodded back and picked himself up from the floor, breathing hard. He felt his backside gingerly.

The door latch lifted with a quiet click. Everyone whirled around. The door swung open and Reverend Jewett entered at his usual dignified pace.

The minister alone had made no attempt at disguise: he wore his usual starched black coat and trousers, and his face was unpainted. He surveyed the wreckage of the taproom with raised brows.

The young officer, Lieutenant Hurley, stepped forward stiffly. "What is the meaning of this ...?" he began in his elegantly accented English, but Tom Wheeler shoved him unceremoniously toward the open door.

"No time to chat now, your lordship," Tom said with a grin. "Out you go, and keep your tongue between your teeth or we'll all be keeping each other company in irons."

"Wait!" commanded the Reverend, his head tilted toward the door. Everyone stood listening with drawn breath. The sound of footsteps pattered outside, quiet footsteps hastening along the road, drawing closer.

Another ragged man burst into the room, his face painted like the others with stripes of red and black. Lemuel recognized him at once: a stooped figure with a long, skinny neck who could only be Bill Tarr.

"Reverend!" Bill panted. "There's a group of Gloucester folk coming up the shore road, coming fast! We can't go that way."

"Let's go straight down to the harbor, then," said Mr. Pool. "We'll commandeer a boat."

"There's guards all along the Neck," Captain Haskell objected. "We'd never get past them."

"They'll be on us in a minute," Bill warned, sticking his head out the door to survey the roadway. The distant chorus of a sea chantey rolled though the night. Lemuel recognized a tune that the fishermen often bawled around the taproom fire: *It's a damned tough life, full of toil and strife, we fishermen undergo ...*

"Up the hill," said the Reverend briskly. "It's the only way clear. Up the hill to the church."

The Sandy Bay men bundled the prisoners out into the road as the Reverend stood holding the door wide. The singers were closer now, bellowing the song into the night: *But we don't give a damn, when the gale is done, how hard the winds did blow!*

Reverend Jewett paused in the doorway to cast a glance over his shoulder at the trussed-up, struggling guards. His pale blue eyes met Lemuel's. The minister gave him a sharp, unsmiling nod, then strode out the door after his flock.

Lemuel ran across the room, avoiding the blindfolded sentries that littered the floor. He opened the door a crack and watched the group race past the darkened houses and up the hill to the moonlit church until the last of the ragged figures disappeared safely inside the big double doors. Relief flowed over him like warm rain.

No sooner did the doors swing shut than a troop of reeling Gloucestermen staggered by the tavern, their arms around each other's shoulders. *We're homeward bound from the fishing ground, on a good ship taut and free, and we don't give a damn when we drink our rum* ... The song faded into the darkness as they passed. Lemuel noiselessly closed the door.

His bare feet made no sound on the wooden floor as he trotted upstairs. He paused to listen cautiously outside his mother's bedroom and was relieved to hear peaceful snores. Pulling on his trousers, he grabbed his jacket and shoes, then tiptoed back down the stairs and crossed the taproom, stepping carefully over the wriggling bodies of the guards. He opened the now-unguarded front door, stepped outside into the moonlight, and shut the door quietly behind him.

CHAPTER 12

Lemuel sat shivering on the harbor pier. The cold of the granite blocks seeped though his wool trousers, and there were goose bumps on his arms. He longed for the morning sun to rise and thaw him out. In the west, behind the splintered church tower, faint pinpricks of stars were still visible, but over the ocean the horizon had a tinge of pink. Distant on the gray sea, the frigate seemed to be biding its time. He could see the movements of tiny figures on the deck.

Lemuel wiggled his freezing toes inside his thin leather shoes. They were a bit too small, a fact he hadn't yet mentioned to his mother—shoes were so expensive these days. His empty stomach growled. He thought longingly of his warm bed and the fried eggs his mother used to make for breakfast on the farm; he was so hungry that even chowder might possibly taste good. But he wasn't going anywhere near the tavern till he was quite sure that the coast was clear.

The fishing boats rocked to and fro as the tide crept into the enclosed basin of the harbor. A movement in the clear water caught his eye, down below the pier where small fish darted and tiny green crabs scuttled through a forest of waving rockweed. A huge, insect-like creature with monstrous claws crawled over the sea bottom. He stared at the ungainly shape clambering over mooring stones speckled with constellations of pink starfish. Then he realized the thing must be a lobster, which he had occasionally seen cooked and on a plate but never alive.

Lying flat on his stomach, he became absorbed in watching a battle between the lobster and a tiny, belligerent crab. He was mentally cheering on the crab, which had just nipped one of the lobster's toes, when a footstep scraped on the granite beside him. He turned his head. Black-stockinged feet in silver-buckled shoes stood on the pier next to him. Reverend Jewett's stern face looked down from on high.

"Idling, young man?" the Reverend demanded. "Slothfulness is one of the seven deadly sins, especially in the young."

Lemuel scrambled to his feet, forgetting his fear of the Reverend. "What's afoot—," he began, but the minister waved aside his eager question.

"Come along, young man, there's work to be done." The Reverend held something white in his hand—a rolled-up piece of linen. "Bear a hand and row me out to the frigate."

Lemuel frowned at the white cloth. "We're not going to surrender, are we?"

The Reverend ignored this question, too. "Hop to it, lad," he said, pointing to Bill's small dory moored at the base of the pier. "The oars are in the shed, over there."

"But ... I don't think I'd be very good at rowing, sir," Lemuel objected. "I, er ... might need to practice a bit."

"No time like the present," the Reverend observed. "Move."

The British vessel had seemed as small as a toy, anchored out in the deep water of the bay. But as they drew closer, bobbing up and down in the little fishing boat, the tall masts, spider-webbed with rigging, stretched high over their heads. There seemed to be more cannons than ever.

Reverend Jewett sat silently in the dory's stern, apparently oblivious to Lemuel's struggles with the oars. The sun was just above the horizon, and the line where the pale morning sky met the dark sea was as straight as if drawn with a ruler. The minister unrolled the white bit of cloth and waved it over his head as they zigzagged across the waves in the brightening day.

An officer with a jaunty cocked hat hailed them with a distant shout. "Who goes there? State your business!"

"I have matters to discuss with the captain," the Reverend called back.

"What do you want, fellow?"

"I have business to discuss with the captain," repeated the Reverend, unruffled.

"What is your business?" bawled the officer, red in the face.

"I will discuss that with the captain," said Reverend Jewett in the voice he used in the pulpit, every word distinct.

The man threw his hands in the air and turned away. Another man appeared at the rail, his cocked hat edged with gold lace.

"Come aboard, sir," the captain called, and his voice echoed as clearly as the Reverend's.

Lemuel managed to steer the dory close to the frigate. A

wave picked up the little boat, shoving it toward the frigate's side, and though Lemuel battled with the oars, the dory hit the ship with a resounding crash. Roars of laughter came from the deck above. "Whole Yank navy's attacking us, lads!" a sailor called. "Man the guns!"

"No need to shoot, just drop a cannonball on their 'eads!" cried another. Lemuel ground his teeth as he struggled with the long oars.

A rope ladder clattered down. The Reverend tied the mooring line of the dory to the ladder, his long fingers weaving a complicated knot. "Stay here," he ordered. He climbed swiftly upward, negotiating the swaying ladder with surprising skill, and his black coattails disappeared over the side. Lemuel managed to ship the dripping oars, then drew a deep breath and settled down to wait.

He drummed his fingers on the oar handles, inspected his blistered palms, and fidgeted on the hard, narrow seat. His empty stomach rumbled in protest as the wavelets bounced the boat up and down. No further sound came from the ship.

He looked nervously out at the water and noticed a dark shape approaching the dory, just below the surface, drifting toward him like the shadow of a cloud. Lemuel frowned up at the clear sky, then looked back at the mysterious shape that was drawing ever closer.

The shadow turned swiftly. He realized it must be an enormous school of fish, fathoms below; thousands upon thousands of fish, all moving together like a flock of blackbirds swooping over a cornfield. *Only a lot of fish,* he told himself—there really were no such things as sea serpents. The shape disappeared under the boat, then appeared again; it circled around, moving faster. *What the sea wants ...*

He grasped the bottom rung of the ladder, swung out of the dory, and scampered up toward the deck as fast as he could go.

The climb was easier the second time. He clambered over the deck rail as he had only two nights ago, glancing warily about. In daylight, he could see more of the frigate's impressive bulk. Unlike the Sandy Bay fishing boats, which were piled with tangled lines, hooks, fish heads, and buckets of bait, the frigate's deck was ordered and tidy: ropes neatly coiled, brass trim gleaming. A half-dozen seamen in colorful kerchiefs were crouched in a line, scrubbing the planks of the already spotless deck. They looked up and eyed him, grinning.

In front of the mainmast, the minister was facing the captain, holding the white cloth at his side. "Yes, I will honor your flag of truce and parley with you," the captain said, looking the Reverend up and down with a perplexed expression. "And what is the purpose of this visit?"

The Reverend lowered his voice. "There are matters to be discussed that could possibly be to our mutual benefit. Might we adjourn to a more private spot?"

The captain raised his brows and studied the minister for a long moment. Then he nodded abruptly and gestured for his visitor to follow him. The curious gaze of the sailors felt cold on Lemuel's back, and he quietly scuttled behind the two men, wondering nervously if the captain would remember him.

The captain led the way to a square opening in the deck and descended steep steps. After the morning brightness, the hot, airless space was pitch black at first, and Lemuel cracked his shin on something hard. Gradually his eyes got used to the dark. The ceiling was so low that he could easily touch it, and the tall minister had to bend low under the beams. A smell of tar and mildew filled the narrow passageways.

The captain led the way to a narrow cabin. A square table covered with charts and brass instruments filled the center of the room, and long, low windows let in slanting sunbeams. There were two stiff-backed chairs, but the captain didn't invite his guests to sit.

"Well, sir?" the captain demanded. He looked the Reverend up and down, ignoring Lemuel. "Who are you and what is your authority?"

"I am the Reverend David Jewett, of the First Congregational Church of the parish of Sandy Bay." The minister gave a slight bow.

"I beg your pardon?" said the captain, leaning forward as if to hear better. "Did you say that you are the reverend of a church?"

"Yes, sir. I am the pastor of the First Congregational Church."

"Are you?" the captain inquired blandly, raising his eyebrows. "A reverend! Well, I'll be damned. And what may you be doing so far from your church, Reverend?"

"I am in search of some of my flock," answered Jewett.

"Ah, your flock," said the captain with a humorless smile.

"Some of them seem to have strayed from the path of duty, I fear. They were all fast asleep when my men captured them."

"Ah, were they?" said the Reverend, in a tone of mild interest. "Perhaps this will be a salutary lesson for them, then. The point of this discussion, however, is that we seem to have returned the favor."

"Have you, indeed?" the captain said. He pulled out a chair and sat down at the small table. "You've captured the landing barge?"

"In a manner of speaking," replied Jewett, also sitting down, uninvited. "The boat sank when your men fired their gun at our church tower. The recoil of the cannon apparently sprung a plank."

"Indeed!" The captain's face was stern. "I see. And what's the butcher's bill, pray?"

"I beg your pardon?" The minister leaned forward, frowning.

"How many were killed?"

"Ah. Well, by God's grace, they are all unharmed," said Jewett. "Some of my parishioners rescued them from the water. They are prisoners, but are well treated."

The captain regarded the Reverend with eyebrows raised high. "And what assurance do I have of this?" he demanded.

"It's true, sir," Lemuel spoke up. "They're all well. My mother was afraid they might catch their deaths, but she wrapped them up warm."

The captain stared at him with astonishment, as if one of the chairs had spoken. "Wrapped them up warm? Who the devil are you, boy?"

"Lemuel Brooks, sir. My mother owns the tavern where the soldiers are—well, where they were, anyway. She made them her rum punch, too. It's very good for chills and especially for—"

"Hold your tongue," said the captain briskly. "Boys should be seen and not heard." Lemuel subsided.

The captain studied the Americans. His mouth twitched. "Rum punch, and wrapped them up warm, if you please," he remarked to no one in particular, then turned to the minister. "And where are my men now?"

"In the church," said Reverend Jewett. "For safekeeping. All well."

There was a silence. Lemuel tried to read the captain's expression, but the face under the gold and blue cocked hat remained grim.

"Well," said the captain finally. "The honors of war would appear to be about even. As I recall, we have nine of your ... flock in custody, and the complement of the barge was eight marines and an officer."

"Precisely." Jewett inclined his head. "I see you are thinking along the same lines as myself."

"An exchange, man for man," said the captain. "That seems straightforward enough."

"Not quite," said the Reverend. Lemuel stared at him in disbelief. The minister sat erect in his chair, his face calm. "I'm afraid we couldn't consider the possibility of an exchange unless you agreed to a condition."

"A condition?" The captain studied the Reverend with cold

blue eyes. Lemuel remembered rumors of keelhauling and the cat-o'-nine tails and wondered if the captain would order them both to be flogged. But the captain blinked, then took off his gold-laced hat and scratched his head. "A condition," he repeated. "And what might that be?"

"That you agree to give Sandy Bay fishermen liberty to ply their trade in these waters, unmolested."

The ship rocked gently as the silence lengthened. Lemuel held his breath. Finally, the captain replaced his cocked hat. "Are you aware, sir," he asked slowly, "how many guns this frigate carries?"

"I believe Colonel Appleton observed thirty-eight," replied the Reverend.

"That is correct," said the captain. "Am I correct in assuming that the only cannon in Sandy Bay are at the bottom of the harbor?"

"Quite correct," returned Jewett.

The captain nodded briskly. "Very well," he said. "An even exchange of prisoners. And the *Nymph* will not molest Sandy Bay craft engaged in the fishing trade henceforth." He stood and held out his hand. "I give you my word of honor," he added. "And I never broke it in my life."

Reverend Jewett rose to his feet, and the two of them shook hands to seal the bargain.

Lemuel was getting the hang of rowing. The dory's path back toward the harbor was nearly straight. As he strained at the oars, he watched the frigate warily, but it was still quietly moored. The sun was well above the horizon, the breeze was warm, and it looked as if it was going to be a nice day.

"I think you've done it, sir," Lemuel said to the Reverend as they neared the harbor. He rowed with growing confidence through the gentle swells.

The Reverend shook his head, staring past Lemuel at the quiet town. The row of houses and shops was lit by the morning sun, and threads of smoke trickled from the chimneys. "It must be seven o'clock or later by now. Our friend Colonel Appleton returned to Gloucester for the night, but I imagine he will go to the tavern shortly to inspect the prisoners. He may not be pleased with what he finds."

"Guess not," said Lemuel with a grin, remembering the trussed-up sentries piled on the floor. "So how do we ...?"

"Save your breath for rowing," the minister advised. "Time and tide wait for no man."

Lemuel rowed, panting, past the rocky tip of Bearskin Neck. The ruins of the watchtower were still sending up wisps of smoke, and crabs were probably nibbling the cannons in the cold water below. In front of the fort's smoke-stained granite blocks, a figure stood watching them, hands on hips, long skirts flapping in the breeze like sails, and Lemuel felt his heart sink. His mother was waiting.

He rowed the rest of the way as fast as he could go. The currents were tricky at the opening to the harbor, where the water flowed through a narrow channel between granite boulders, and Lemuel winced as the borrowed dory crunched against a rock. He shot a glance at the Reverend, but he appeared not to have noticed, and Lemuel rowed on, trying not to imagine what Bill would say. He maneuvered awkwardly with the oars as the dory careened off schooners and tall sloops, but he finally succeeded in reaching the iron ring in the pier's side that was the dory's mooring spot.

Reverend Jewett nimbly climbed up the ladder. "A fair job of rowing, sir," he said over his shoulder. "Keep up your practice."

"Now what do we do?" asked Lemuel, but the minister was already out of earshot, walking as fast as he could without actually running.

Lemuel tied the boat to the rusty iron ring, his fingers fumbling with the knot. He clambered up the ladder, then hesitated on the pier, not sure which way to go. The Reverend disappeared around the corner, heading for the center of town. From the other direction, his mother hastened down the road toward him. Lemuel chewed his lip, considering. Danger lay on either hand.

He took a deep breath and scurried after the minister, heading for Dock Square and the steep road to the church.

CHAPTER 13

Lemuel followed Reverend Jewett at a distance as far as Dock Square. Clusters of yawning militiamen were gathered at the pump, splashing their faces and gossiping. The minister paced calmly under the elms and past the Pool mansion, nodding benevolently at the sentries as he passed.

All seemed quiet, but Lemuel took a cautious detour, just in case. He ran along a strip of muddy beach till he came to a deserted cove, then climbed back toward the town on a winding, rocky path. He had discovered the little cove on a berry-picking expedition; the narrow way was tangled with thornbushes and raspberry brambles, and he struggled up the brushy path while thorns clawed at his sleeves and catbriers scratched his legs. He raced up the hill, through the back gardens of the cottages that lined the steep road, and emerged on the roadway just below the church.

Once there, he slowed to avoid attracting attention. He buttoned his brown wool jacket and straightened his collar, then strolled along, whistling, trying to look as though he was on his way to school. Housewives were opening shutters and sweeping off doorsteps as the rising sun shone on the peaceful yards and gardens, where chickens browsed sleepily and pumpkins and yellow squash glowed in the morning light.

Lemuel reached the churchyard, which was still strewn with splinters and shards of wood from the damaged tower. Stepping over the debris, he climbed up the granite steps of the church. He paused on the top step to glance over his shoulder, half-expecting to see a furious Colonel Appleton and hundreds of Gloucester militiamen pursuing him up the hill. But the road was empty, except for a couple of white geese strolling along, prospecting for insects and peering hopefully into each puddle.

Then he saw his mother come from the harbor road into Dock Square; she paused at the pump, shading her eyes and looking around. Lemuel pushed the big church door open a crack and hastily slipped inside.

The silence filled his ears. The high-roofed, wide space was deserted: the rows of tall wooden pews were bare, the pulpit empty. Rows of sconces lined the walls of the church, but no cheerful candles flickered in them. The rippled glass window-panes let slanting bars of sunlight into the dim expanse.

A trickle of voices sounded from the front of the church. Lemuel took a cautious step, and his foot on the flagstones made a whispering echo. He crept down the center aisle, the long, narrow windows and high ceiling making him feel as small as a mouse in a pantry.

The voices came through the door of the small vestry room, just behind the pulpit. Lemuel tiptoed in back of the altar, shocked at his own boldness in trespassing on this forbidden territory, where no one but the Reverend ever set foot. He went silently up to the vestry door and peeped inside.

The Reverend, Ebenezer Pool, and a dozen other men were huddled together in hot argument. The Sandy Bay men had washed the paint from their faces and taken off their ragged disguises; the fishermen were wearing their usual pea jackets and trousers, while Ebenezer Pool had resumed his brass-buttoned frock coat and beaver hat. They were surrounded by the British soldiers in their red coats and water-stained white breeches. Everyone seemed to be talking at once.

"Let's just head down the hill to the harbor and jump in the *Eliza*," said Tom Wheeler, raising his voice over the noise. "But we've got to go now! Appleton won't sit around and twiddle his thumbs once he finds that the fish are out of the net."

"But what if he's already found out?" asked Captain Haskell. "There might be a troop of militia on their way here this instant."

"Well, there might be," Ebenezer Pool agreed. "So let's go before they get here!"

"Wait a minute!" said Bill Tarr. "What'll Appleton say if he sees all nine of 'em walking down the street in a row? He's not an idiot. We can't just parade down the street to the harbor."

"We can't all go in a group," said a gray-haired soldier. "It would draw too much attention. But if we went one or two at a time ..."

"We must stay together, Sanders." Lieutenant Hurley looked older in his gold-laced uniform. "Isn't there any other way than the main street to get down to the boats?" he demanded.

Tom shook his head. "Not without climbing over rocks and crossing the beach in full view of everyone," he said.

The argument continued, but Lemuel stopped listening. He looked at each of the enemy soldiers, studying their faces: Hill, the red-headed young man, pale under his freckles; the small and wiry soldier, Martin; the tall, stocky Sergeant Archer, who was as big and broad-shouldered as Tom Wheeler. The gray-haired soldier, Sanders, was scratching a nose as red-veined and weather-beaten as Bill Tarr's. Lemuel remembered the soldiers standing in his mother's kitchen after shedding their red coats, and how they had suddenly looked like ordinary Sandy Bay folk.

"Nay, we can't go out there, 'tis broad daylight now," said Hill in his rough Scottish burr. "We'd stand out like crows in a blizzard."

"Silence in the ranks!" snapped the officer. "We'll fight them if we have to."

"There'll be no fighting here, brethren," said Reverend Jewett. "We shall find another way."

There was a silence. Through the open window came a trill of morning birdsong. Lemuel took a deep breath and spoke into the quiet. "It doesn't matter if anyone sees them," he said, "as long as they take off their coats."

Everyone started, then turned to stare at him. "What's that, lad?" said Sergeant Archer.

"We're busy here, my boy," said Mr. Pool, not unkindly. "Clear away home, now."

"No, let him speak." The Reverend frowned. "What do you mean?"

"Well, they ... they look just like anyone else, really, without the coats," Lemuel stammered before his courage could give out. "They could just be fishermen, going down to the boats as usual ... going with some of us, maybe ..." His voice faded into the echoing stillness of the church. Everyone stared at him. The silence stretched thin.

Then a voice spoke from behind him, a woman's voice that was very familiar. "Come and take a walk, my dear?"

Lemuel spun around. His mother stood just behind him.

She gave him a glance with narrowed eyes, pursing her lips. "I'll deal with you later, sir," she promised in a low voice. "Making me chase you all over creation." Then she stepped forward, patting her untidy red curls into place, and smiled at Sergeant Archer. "Would you walk with me as far as the harbor, sir?" she asked him, holding out her arm invitingly as Lemuel's brows rose high in astonishment.

Archer blinked at her, then looked uncertainly at Lieutenant Hurley. The officer gave a sharp nod. "She's right! And so's the boy. Off with your coat!"

Sanders nudged Archer with a broad grin. "Go on, you lucky sod," he said. "You're always the chap the ladies fancy."

Archer pulled off his scarlet coat and tossed it on the floor as Tom Wheeler stripped off his rough blue pea jacket. "Here," Tom said, holding out the fishy-smelling garment. "See if it fits."

"Thank'ee, mate," said Archer, and struggled into the jacket. He held out his arms, regarding the worn sleeves admiringly. "Perfect fit," he said. "Nice and warm, I'll be bound."

His white breeches, stained and dirty, seemed to blend with the old coat. Tom handed him a woolen cap to complete the figure of a ragged fisherman. Archer swept Mrs. Brooks a gallant bow. "May I have the honor of your company, ma'am?"

She took his arm with a flirtatious tilt of her chin. Lemuel stood watching openmouthed as the pair marched arm-in-arm down the center aisle of the empty church. They went out through the big double doors.

Tom turned to the other soldiers in a business-like manner. "All right, lads!" He pointed at random. "You four—you and you and you two—you're my crew." Bill Tarr and Captain Haskell pulled off their pea jackets and wool caps and traded clothes with two of the soldiers. Ebenezer Pool took off his high-crowned beaver hat and regarded it doubtfully, then put it back on his head.

The Reverend opened a large wooden cupboard that took up one corner of the vestry and pulled out an armful of ragged shirts and coats. "For the poor and needy," he said. "The Lord will provide." He distributed the clothing among the rest of the soldiers. They put on the tattered garments and pulled moth-eaten wool caps down over their ears.

"Come on, then, lads," said Tom. "We're making for the harbor to head out after cod—no time to spare. Look sharp!" He shooed the ragged figures out of the vestry and along the aisle between the pews. "You're in luck, shipmates, you've been promoted, you have. You're Sandy Bay fishermen."

Bill Tarr straightened his back and looked around. His eye fell on Lieutenant Hurley, who was examining a ragged jacket with distaste, and he beckoned to the young British officer. "Come along, lad, you can do my rowing for me—I'm not as young as I was. I'll take you instead of this young jackanapes here," he added, elbowing Lemuel in the ribs. "Pretty good as ballast, but he talks too much."

The Lieutenant hesitated, then struggled out of his tight-fitting coat.

"Pick up your feet, boy, and look alive, or you'll get the rope's end," Bill growled. Lemuel met the Lieutenant's eye in sympathy as Bill prodded the young officer out the vestry door. Bill's gravelly voice could be heard giving advice on how to bait a hook as the pair went down the church steps.

The Reverend nodded calmly to Ebenezer, who took a deep breath and turned to the three remaining Englishmen. "Well, Sanders, is it?" he said to the gray-headed soldier.

"Aye, John Sanders, sir." The man buttoned a stained blue jacket up to his chin. "Shall we have a go?" He pulled a ragged stocking cap low on his forehead.

"I suppose so," said Ebenezer. He looked at the other two soldiers. "What're your names?" he asked.

"Martin, sir, Will Martin." The small man touched his cap.

"Ezekiel Hill, sir."

"Well, I'm Ebenezer Pool. Pleased to make your acquaintance." He shrugged. "Well, come on, then, no help for it. You're my crew, and we're off for cod, mind." He walked down the aisle and through the tall church doors. The others followed.

A cool draft blew from the inside of the church onto Lemuel's back as the little group stood on the church steps. "Good luck, Eb," said Captain Haskell, his pleasant brown eyes grave.

"Off you go, lads," said the Reverend to Ebenezer Pool

and his fictitious crew. "And may God have you in His holy keeping." The Reverend and Haskell withdrew into the silence of the church. The big doors closed softly behind them.

"All right, then," said Ebenezer, looking down at Lemuel beside him on the step. "Clear away out of this now, boy."

"But can't I come with—"

"No, no, cut away home." He tipped his tall beaver hat to Lemuel, then settled the hat firmly back on his head and trotted down the steps. The soldiers followed, wordlessly touching their caps to Lemuel as they passed.

Half-glad, half-sorry to be left behind, he stood to watch the procession make its way down the rutted road: first his mother and Sergeant Archer, already halfway down the hill; then Tom and his crew, followed by Bill Tarr, stumping along with the Lieutenant, and then Mr. Pool and his men. The sun was peeping over the trees that lined the street, casting long shadows that striped the road, and the leaves moved gently in the morning breeze. Past the harbor, the sea stretched like a blue wall on the horizon. The Union Jack fluttered from the mast of the waiting frigate.

Lemuel surveyed the escape route with an anxious eye. The harbor wasn't far—he could easily run the distance in a minute or two. The fugitives had only to go down the hill, cross Dock Square, walk a few yards down Bearskin Neck, and then turn left by the tavern onto the harbor path. But the sun was well up now, and the square was filling with people. A group of Gloucester militiamen were having a morning wash at the pump, their muskets stacked nearby.

An abrupt shout sounded from the tavern, at the bottom of the hill, and instantly all heads swiveled in that direction. The taproom door burst open, and a tall, uniformed figure emerged. Colonel Appleton stood in the road, looking wildly from side to side, the taproom door swinging on its hinges behind him. Ebenezer and his followers halted as if turned to stone.

"Sound the alarm!" Appleton cried. One of the soldiers in the square snatched up a drum, and the militiamen leaped for their muskets. The harsh rattle of the drum made a dozen guards come running from the harbor, weapons in hand. The Colonel shouted orders, and the guards scattered to begin the search, banging on the doors of houses and shops that lined the square.

Colonel Appleton drew his sword. The long blade flashed in the sun. Then he turned and strode purposefully up the road, heading straight for the church.

CHAPTER 14

Colonel Appleton barreled up the pleasant, tree-lined street at full speed, aiming directly for Sergeant Archer. Lemuel's mother grasped the arm of her companion, glancing from side to side in desperation. There were no side streets handy between them and the Colonel, no short cuts, nowhere to hide. The distance was narrowing rapidly. Watching frozen from the church steps, Lemuel squeezed his eyes shut, but immediately opened them again.

Archer had stopped dead in the middle of the road, but Mrs. Brooks gave his arm a yank and dragged him on. They drew nearer to the Colonel, and nearer, as Lemuel held his breath; then they had passed each other, the Colonel not giving the pair as much as a backward glance.

The four men with Tom Wheeler passed the Colonel next. Appleton slowed as the little group hurried by with shoulders hunched and faces averted. He stopped in the middle of the road and turned to stare after them. Lieutenant Hurley, coming in his turn down the street, nearly collided with the Colonel, but the young man managed to skip nimbly out of the way. Bill Tarr, close behind, didn't dodge as quickly, and he and the Colonel crashed full into each other.

Colonel Appleton staggered, red in the face, but managed to keep his balance. He opened his mouth, but Bill didn't give him a chance to speak. The old fisherman leaned forward and shook a finger under the Colonel's nose. "Take in some canvas, there, and watch where you're going, young man," he scolded. "No respect for your elders!" Bill snorted loudly, then brushed past the speechless Colonel. He scurried off toward the harbor, moving faster than Lemuel had ever seen him go.

Appleton stood, his sword held low, to watch the retreating figures hurry down the road. Lemuel held his breath again, but the Colonel swung around and resumed his charge up the hill. Ebenezer Pool and the others were still halted just a few steps down from the church, watching the Colonel storm up the road. Ebenezer barked, "Come on!" to his reluctant crew and stepped forward.

Appleton looked up and saw them coming. But instead of brushing past, he planted himself in the middle of the road, hands on hips, and awaited their approach. The Colonel's thin face was working with fury, brows drawn low. Lemuel scooted behind the thick trunk of a nearby elm tree to stay out of range of those cold eyes.

"Good day, sir," Ebenezer said in a casual voice. "You're abroad early this morning."

"Not early enough, I fear," returned Appleton in a voice that shook with fury. "I am given to understand that the prisoners have been freed."

"You astonish me, sir!" Ebenezer cried, and Lemuel, listening with all his might, admired his authentically surprised tone of voice. "The prisoners have escaped?" asked Ebenezer.

"Not 'escaped,' Mr. Pool," said Appleton, biting off each word. "They've been freed—the sentries overpowered and trussed up, and the prisoners gone! By God, when I find out who was asleep on watch, I'll stretch their necks for them." His lips set in a grim line.

"Why, the British must have—"

"Not the British, sir. Local men. Hooligans dressed in stocking caps and painted faces."

"Painted faces?" said Ebenezer. "Why, bless me, it sounds like the Boston Tea Party."

"Not in the least, sir!" Appleton shouted. "These are traitors, criminals—they'll swing from the gallows if I lay my hand on them. Follow me! We must look into this matter at once."

"I would like to help you, sir, but I regret—," Ebenezer began.

Appleton swung back, eyebrows raised as high as they would go. "I beg your pardon?" he said with quiet menace.

"I would like to assist, but unfortunately affairs call me. I am about to embark on an expedition ... er ... a fishing expedition ..."

"Fishing?" Appleton's gaze raked the crew. Hill shuffled his feet, his blue eyes wide, and Martin glanced furtively toward the harbor. Lemuel hoped that neither of them would break and run for it. "Fishing!" Appleton exclaimed. "When matters of national importance—"

Ebenezer interrupted the Colonel for once. "I regret I cannot be of assistance," he said firmly. "But as you can see, my crew is ready and the tide will not wait. I'm sure you'll find there's a reasonable explanation for all this, Colonel." He tipped his hat as he turned away. "I should take it up with the committee."

Appleton surveyed the crew. His heavy-lidded eyes had a wolflike gleam. "What's your vessel?" he demanded, glaring at one of the soldiers at random. It was the red-headed boy, Hill, who gazed back in terror, his lips clamped shut. Lemuel knew that if the soldier opened his mouth and spoke one word in his broad accent, the game was up.

"Well?" Appleton said irritably. "Speak when you're spoken to, boy. Are you an idiot?"

Hill said nothing. His wide eyes and quivering, long face made Lemuel think of a sheep.

"Well?" shouted Appleton, stepping forward and thrusting his face inches from the young man's nose. "Speak up, curse you!"

Hill's lips parted, and he drew a quavering breath. Ebenezer Pool clenched his fists, as though weighing the chances of knocking Appleton down and making a run for it. The militiamen in the square were looking curiously in their direction. There seemed no possibility of escape. Mr. Pool and the soldiers were caught like sheep surrounded by wolves.

Something about the thought of sheep and wolves made Lemuel's mind reach far back—back to the days when he was little enough to sit on his father's knee; his mother said he was too young for battle tales, so his father had told him an old, old story—about a shepherd and a flock of sheep, and a boy who cried a warning of a wolf that wasn't there. ...

His voice broke into the silence, clear and shrill. There was no time to plan his words; he just shouted out the first desperate thought that popped into his head. "The British!"

The men all spun around. Lemuel ran up to them and gazed eagerly at the tall colonel. "Sir!" he exclaimed. "The British! They're landing!"

"What's that, boy?" cried the Colonel. "The British! Where?"

Lemuel blinked. "In the ... in the cove!" he said. "That way!" He waved an arm vaguely toward the ocean.

"The cove! There's a hundred coves along the bay!" The Colonel grasped Lemuel's collar and gave him a shake. "Which one?"

"Haddock Cove," replied Lemuel promptly, recalling his last bowl of chowder.

"Haddock Cove?" Appleton cried. "Where the devil's that?"

Lemuel's powers of invention gave out. He jerked loose from the Colonel's grip, leaving a white shred of collar clenched in the man's fist, and sped away down the hill toward the square.

"You there, boy, wait!" Colonel Appleton roared. "How many troops? What force? Stop, I say!"

Lemuel ignored the voice that thundered after him. He sped down the hill, waving both arms at the militiamen in the square as he approached. "Hurry!" he called. "This way!" He raced toward the shore road that skirted the bay.

Appleton came down the hill at a long-legged, awkward run, shouting to the guards. "Lively, men! I want a hundred men in that cove, double quick!" Drums rolled and a bugle sounded. Lemuel put his head down and ran in earnest.

Breath tore in and out of his lungs; his feet hammered on the road. A stitch cut into his side like a knife blade. Behind him he could hear a rising tide of shouted orders and the thud of boots as the pursuers gained on him.

He fled down the shore road, retracing the detour he had taken half an hour earlier, and skidded to a halt at the head of the winding gravel footpath that led toward the sea. The horde of red-faced, panting militiamen pounded toward him, muskets in hand. He pointed to the water. "That way! Hurry!"

The troop of Gloucestermen, led by the Colonel with drawn sword, rushed down the narrow path, cursing as they slipped and skidded on the rocks. Lemuel cheered them on, waving his arms like a windmill. More and more soldiers raced past him.

Finally the stream of Gloucestermen ceased, and the last of them disappeared from his view down the steep path. A faint sound of words his mother would never allow him to say drifted to his ears as the militiamen struggled through the thorns and brambles. Lemuel sank down on a handy rock, his knees suddenly weak with relief.

As soon as his heart slowed its pounding, he stood up. His chest was still heaving and he couldn't run any more, but he trotted as quickly as possible back the way he had come. He crossed the empty square, hurrying down to the harbor, and was just in time to see Mr. Pool and his three companions climb into a large dory.

Ebenezer Pool waved to him, and Sanders, Martin, and Hill jauntily tipped their ragged wool caps. They cast off and rowed for the frigate, all four men bending to the oars.

In the distance, he observed that two other craft had almost reached the ship. Shading his eyes against the sun sparkling on the water, he recognized the outlines of Bill Tarr's dory and Tom Wheeler's graceful *Eliza Jane*.

"Well, sir!" said a stern voice behind him, and he jumped. His mother stood on the pier, hands on hips, studying him with a frown. Then she reached out and grabbed his collar as Colonel Appleton had done, but she was smiling as she shook him gently back and forth. She ruffled his hair, and he grinned up at her.

"Well, sir," she said again, a smile in her eyes, "if it isn't Paul Revere."

CHAPTER 15

Lemuel Brooks leaned over the side of the boat and looked down into the sparkling water of Sandy Bay. There was a fish on the end of his line; he could feel the weight of it as he pulled it in hand over hand, and he smiled as he saw the silver shape, far below, rising through the transparent water.

Hauling in the line was hard work, but Lemuel persevered. Soon the fish was almost level with the surface. But when he stretched out a hand, the big fish gave one last twist and broke free of the hook. Lemuel groaned and leaned over the clear water, watching the fish swim away into blue shadows far below.

The slender craft tilted, the low side sagging near the waves. "Trim her!" snapped Bill. "Sweet Jesus, these landlubbers! How many times do I have to tell you?"

"Oh, belay your fussing," said Tom easily, leaning back in his seat in the stern. "You just like to hear yourself talk. The *Eliza*'s not going to turn turtle like your old tub."

"And what would I tell his mother if he fell in?" demanded Bill. "Sink straight to the bottom, he would, and that'd be the end of him, and good riddance, too. No room for passengers on a fishing craft."

"I wouldn't sink straight to the bottom," Lemuel objected mildly. He was getting used to Bill. "I can swim, after all."

"Swim!" said Bill, staring at him, white eyebrows raised high. Tom stared, too. "Haven't I told you, no Sandy Bay fisherman learns how to swim. Why, he'd be a Jonah, for sure."

"So what?" Lemuel asked absently. "We used to go swimming in the millpond at home all the time." He rebaited his hook with care.

"Ah, Jonahs are old wives' tales," said Tom, a shade uneasily. "Lemuel's no Jonah. He's been some good luck for Sandy Bay. I hear the Colonel's posted guards in the cove for the last three days. They're still looking for those Redcoats." He chuckled. "I suppose someday someone'll tell him there's no such place as Haddock Cove."

Bill scratched his head, chewing his pipe stem. "Still," he said. "Swimming! Well, it don't matter, anyway, I suppose," he added, shrugging. "What the sea wants, she'll take."

They fished awhile, in a silence broken only by the slap of the ripples on the side of the *Eliza Jane* and the soft rustle of the furled sail. They were far out past Halibut Point and could barely hear the murmur of the waves breaking on Bearskin Neck. Cormorants fished lazily alongside the boat, snagging small silver herring with their long beaks. The birds tossed them up in the air as though flipping a coin to catch the fish headfirst and swallow them whole. A pile of good-size cod lay flapping in the bottom of the boat. Bill and Tom seemed to haul them in as fast as they could rebait their hooks, but Lemuel's line dangled loosely in his hand.

Finally, he felt a slight tug and immediately jerked on the rope.

"Too fast," said Tom. "Got to set her."

Sure enough, Lemuel felt the line go slack again.

"Try again, and bait properly this time," said Bill.

Lemuel hauled up his long line and inspected the empty hook sadly, then reached into the slimy bucket of clams. He rebaited and cast the line once more over the side.

The warm sun made the fishy smell from the bucket even stronger, and he raised his head to get a whiff of fresh air. As he looked up, his jaw dropped and he gasped aloud.

"What is it, mate?" said Tom without looking up. "Put a hook in your thumb?"

Lemuel felt his mouth go dry. "The ... the British ...," he stammered.

Bill snorted. "That joke's old as yesterday's fish," he said. "Don't be trying that one on ..." His voice broke off as he looked up, and he gasped, too.

Tom glanced at Bill's horrified face and spun around to stare across the water.

From behind the rocks of Halibut Point glided a tall ship, the masts laden with white sails. Lemuel recognized the graceful lines of the frigate, the gilding on the prow, and the black line of gunports stretching across the side. Hidden by the point of land, the ship had sailed close in before they had noticed it.

The frigate began to turn slowly. "They've seen us," said Tom in a low voice. The great sails filled in the breeze, and the ship skimmed silently toward them, picking up speed. Tom and Bill looked at each other, their faces pale.

"They won't hurt us," said Lemuel with confidence. "I told you, the Reverend made it a condition."

Tom pulled at his beard. "I don't know," he said. "It's wartime, after all. They're always short of men for their blasted navy."

"A craft like this could be worth a lot of prize money," Bill muttered.

The ship came closer, bearing down on them like a storm cloud. "It'll be all right," Lemuel said stoutly, but he reached into his pocket and grasped his lucky stone. "The captain promised that Sandy Bay craft would never be ..." His voice died as the ship approached, heading straight toward them.

Figures lined the deck, red and blue uniforms mixed with the sailors' colored neckerchiefs; the sharp bowsprit was aimed at them like a musket. He remembered the captain's pale eyes and his cold voice: *Am I correct in assuming that the only cannons in Sandy Bay are at the bottom of the harbor?*

Then, with a hiss and rush of waves, the ship veered to one side; the high deck cruised by, the wash making the *Eliza* spin and bob. Faces lined the rail, looking down at them, but there was no time to read their expressions or recognize anyone before the ship surged past.

The roiling water calmed. The frigate faded in the distance. No one spoke as they watched the tall ship's sails blending with the white feathers of clouds on the horizon.

Finally, Lemuel broke the silence. "See?" he said, a slow grin spreading across his face. "I told you!"

Bill Tarr blew out a deep breath. "Well, guess I've had

enough for today," he said, though the boat wasn't half-full of fish. "Let's head for port."

"Why not?" Tom agreed, wiping the sweat off his brow. "I'm about ready to go in." He gave a shaky sigh. "But wait—look to your line, boy!"

Lemuel hadn't noticed the taut line he was holding and was surprised to feel a strong tug.

"Haul in!" Tom said, grabbing at the reel, but Lemuel snatched it away and held on tightly. He strained to pull in yard after yard of icy, dripping rope. The great silver fish rose to the surface and thrashed near the boat. Spray splashed over their heads.

Lemuel let go the line and plunged both arms elbow-deep into the freezing water. He grasped the slimy gills and hauled the green and silver fish over the side of the boat. "Got one!" he said, panting triumphantly.

"Twenty-pounder," said Bill, blowing a wreath of smoke toward him. "Not too bad, for a passenger."

"A nice fat cod!" Tom slapped Lemuel on the back, almost knocking him off his seat.

"Chowder for supper!" said Bill. "Got to clean her first, though," he added. "Mind how I showed you."

Lemuel groaned aloud. But a smile slowly spread across his face, and then he began to laugh. He couldn't help it. Bill and Tom stared at him, obviously wondering what the joke was, but warm laughter bubbled up within him, and he couldn't stop. Suddenly, Tom's deep voice joined in, ringing over the water, mingled with Bill's rusty wheezing laugh. The three of them sat in the bobbing boat and roared with mirth.

Finally, they subsided into chuckles. Lemuel leaned back against the side of the boat, still giggling, and looked up at the mild, wide sky overhead. "I'm hungry!" he said. "Let's go home."

"Home it is!" Tom hauled up the sail, and the white triangle billowed and snapped in the wind. The *Eliza Jane* heeled over, then picked up speed as the wind pushed her along. The little craft churned a white line of foam on the water as they headed home to Sandy Bay.

AFTERWORD

OLD STONE
★ FORT ★

Site of fort erected
by public subscription
as a protection against
British warships during
the war of 1812, captured
in a sneak attack and
dismantled by frigate NYMPH.
Ammunition gone, all nine
seafencibles taken prisoner,
the townsmen hurled rocks,
using their stockings as slings.

Historical Marker on Bearskin Neck,
Rockport, Massachusetts

What Really Happened?

It was the historical marker that interested me in the first place. I always paused to read the big wooden sign on my childhood visits to Cape Ann. I would stand on the windy tip of Bearskin Neck and look over the wide bay, wondering what had happened on that day so long ago. The detail of the stockings fascinated me. I had to admire the indomitable spirit of the townsfolk, who would use just about anything they could get their hands on to fight off invaders.

The War of 1812 is a difficult war to understand. Historians argue to this day over exactly why the war started in the first place. Boundary disputes and trade disagreements caused trouble between Great Britain and the United States, but what really angered New Englanders was the fact that the British sometimes captured American sailors and forced them to join the Royal Navy. Whatever the reasons, by 1812 the United States was fighting mad. The small, new country went to war, for the second time, with the ancient and powerful kingdom of Great Britain, a young minnow challenging a whale.

Bitter fighting raged for two years, and men died on land and sea. Fishermen couldn't go out to fish on an ocean filled with enemy warships, and New Englanders soon began to long for peace. Pressure to end the unpopular war grew, and finally British and American diplomats met in Europe to negotiate a treaty.

They haggled for months over the terms of the peace, debating territorial boundaries, fishing rights, and trade restrictions, as the bloody war continued. And when the diplomats finally signed the Treaty of Ghent that formally ended the war, the articles of the treaty were based on the principle of a return to the *status quo ante bellum*—in other words, the treaty returned conditions to the way they had been before the war began.

So the War of 1812 was a war that changed nothing. But, like all wars, it changed everything for the people who lived through it day by day. The war had an especially harsh impact on Americans, like the folk of Sandy Bay, who drew their living from the sea.

Welcome to Sandy Bay

Sandy Bay is a real place. The little town, now known as Rockport, is located on Cape Ann, a rocky promontory that juts into the Atlantic Ocean on the north shore of Massachusetts. American Indians fished the waters of the bay for thousands of years before the Europeans arrived in 1690. The Tarrs were the first family of English settlers; they established the town at the tip of Cape Ann and were shortly followed by the Pools. They found that the icy water held fish in incredible abundance, plentiful enough to scoop up in baskets from the side of a boat. The Sandy Bay fishermen thrived.

Boats still sail past Bearskin Neck and out into the waters of Sandy Bay. These days, however, most of the vessels carry tourists, not fishermen. There are far fewer fishing craft today than in 1814 because there are far fewer fish, after centuries of tragic and relentless over-fishing. But many sightseers come to explore the historic village, from the tall Old Sloop church on the hill to the fish-drying shacks—now gift shops—on Bearskin Neck. Many of the buildings that made up the village of Sandy Bay during the War of 1812 still stand, including the Ebenezer Pool house in Dock Square, the Sea Fencibles' barracks, and the Punch Bowl Tavern.

Incidentally, the first American sea serpent was reported off Cape Ann, in 1639, and has been sighted several hundreds of times since. Sightings were particularly common in the early 1800s, but the huge monster that was described then hasn't been reported since the 1960s.

Who's Real, Who's Not?

Many of the characters in *The Invasion of Sandy Bay* are real people, although little is known about their personalities, which I have inferred from their actions. Ebenezer Pool, Reverend David Jewett, Tom Wheeler, Captain Benjamin Haskell and the inept Sea Fencibles, the Royal Navy captain, and the narrow-minded bureaucrat Colonel James Appleton—they all really existed. Lemuel Brooks, his mother, and Bill Tarr are invented characters, although their lives are closely based on the actual experiences of people of that time.

How Do We Know What Really Happened?

Most of this story is based on the voluminous writings of Ebenezer Pool. Although only twenty-eight at the time of the invasion, Ebenezer Pool was a leading citizen and also an avid writer, who recorded every detail of life in his beloved town. He saw Sandy Bay change through the course of ninety years and was the town's unofficial historian, recording births and deaths, wars and gales, blizzards and festivals throughout his long life. He was proud to have been not only a witness but also a participant in the events of what was undoubtedly the most exciting night in the history of Sandy Bay.

Ebenezer wasn't the only writer to record the details of the invasion, though. The British captain described the events in the terse, official language of his daily logbook, retained in the archives of the Royal Navy. The *Nymph*'s captain noted the attack, but prudently omitted any mention of the shooting of the church bell and the embarrassing incident of the sinking barge.

In the late 1800s, Caleb Pool, a descendant of Ebenezer, interviewed many eyewitnesses, and their combined memories were set down in a memoir. Decades after the events, three things were clearly remembered by all—the orange glow of flames, the smell of smoke, and the brave, defiant clanging of the church bell.

Other memories were blurred, or improved, with time. One veteran Sea Fencible, reminiscing about the invasion, told a thrilling tale of how he and the other men garrisoned at the fort courageously fought off the attacking Redcoats.

The Invasion

The families of Sandy Bay, like those in the rest of New England, endured hard times as the war affected them economically. But the violence of actual warfare must have seemed as distant as a sail on the horizon. Cape Ann fishermen had a special exemption from militia service, on the grounds that they were "mariners." But in August of 1813, a passing British privateer ship fired a cannonball at the town. No damage was done, but the villagers woke up to the fact that the war had arrived on their very doorstep.

The Sandy Bay folk refused to be cowed by the might of the Royal Navy. Fishermen became militiamen, and a troop called the Sandy Bay Sea Fencibles was mustered, with elaborate uniforms and gleaming bayonets. Soon the town voted to fund the building of an impressive granite fort on the end of Bearskin

Neck. The citizens raised $600 by public subscription—a vast amount of money in a time when the average citizen of Sandy Bay paid about $1.50 per year in taxes.

Though there were constant reports of British vessels off the coast, time passed peacefully for a while. But before dawn on September 8, 1814, the British frigate *Nymph* approached Cape Ann. The *Nymph* captured the crew of a small Sandy Bay fishing boat that was far out to sea and forced the crew to pilot the frigate along Cape Ann's rocky coast and into the bay. The British dropped anchor off Bearskin Neck, unseen by anyone on land. The Sea Fencibles who garrisoned the fort were, to a man, sound asleep.

Two small barges filled with Royal Marines—red-coated soldiers who traveled on Royal Navy vessels to make land assaults—silently rowed toward the shore under cover of a heavy fog. They attacked the town from two sides. The details of the invasion—the capture of the fort, the shooting of the church bell, and the sinking of the British barge—are re-created in this book as recorded by an eyewitness: Ebenezer Pool.

The British attacked, Ebenezer wrote, "about day light in the morning, then very foggy." The invaders "spiked 2 canon and hove them off the breastwork, [and] set fire to the watch house ... the Bell at the meeting house began to ring an alarm to the inhabitants, when the [other] barge whilst passing the end of the pier fired at the Meeting house, deposited a shot in one of the steeple-posts and at the same time they started a butt in the bow of their Barge."

No injuries were recorded on either side during the brief

battle. Since Sandy Bay had no jail, the British were imprisoned in the local tavern and in a nearby house, where they were "well provided for" by the kindhearted Sandy Bay folk.

No one knows who summoned the Gloucester militia, but they did show up, more than a thousand strong. Too late to help fight the foe, Colonel Appleton refused to exchange prisoners with the British, insisting that the matter be referred to a higher authority. The citizens of Sandy Bay begged him to change his mind; those captured by the British were usually kept in extremely harsh conditions and often died.

So the invasion of Sandy Bay really happened.

But What Happened Then?

In the next few days, inhabitants of neighboring towns heard the shocking news of the Sandy Bay attack. But soon, people began to wonder what had really occurred. William Bentley, of the nearby town of Salem, stated in his diary that "the Sandy Bay affair has been variously represented" and reported that a rumor was already afoot that the British prisoners had been "secreted."

In all of Ebenezer Pool's writings—a pile of manuscript that is literally a foot high—nowhere did he give an account of exactly how the British prisoners were freed in the face of Colonel Appleton's flat refusal to consider an exchange. It was an enterprise that was clearly irregular, if not downright treasonable, and perhaps no one wanted to write down the details. Not until fifty years later did a Massachusetts historian record the tradition that the Sandy Bay folk took the law into their own hands: they disguised themselves and used force to free the British from Colonel Appleton's guards, then arranged an exchange that was carried out in secret. My account of the prisoners' flight from the church to the harbor is fiction.

It is history, though, that the *Nymph*'s captain honorably kept his word. "And from that time," Ebenezer wrote, "Whilst stationed off Cape Ann he gave the Boat Fishermen free liberty to fish unmolested."

After the War

The War of 1812 ended only weeks after the invasion of Sandy Bay, in December 1814. The Sandy Bay folk immediately resumed fishing to "great profit." Fishermen ventured ever farther from shore, as far as the Grand Banks off Canada.

The townsfolk retrieved the sunken barge and divided the "small arms and cutlasses" among themselves. "The cannon ... is yet retained as town property," Ebenezer Pool noted with obvious satisfaction, "to be used on fourth of July." The small black cannon is still proudly displayed on the lawn of the Old Sloop church.

The Sandy Bay townsfolk finally became so fed up with their overbearing Gloucester neighbors that they formally seceded from Gloucester in 1840—and the Gloucestermen were doubtless rather glad to see them go. The Sandy Bay folk voted on a new name, and the town was rechristened *Rockport*.

It is my own invention that Reverend Jewett masterminded the rescue. Nothing is known about the Reverend's actions during the invasion. But, although a stern moralist, he was held in such high regard that after his death, many years later in New Hampshire, the citizens of Sandy Bay petitioned to have his remains interred in their town. He is buried in what is now known as the Old Burying Ground under a massive granite monument.

There he rests to this day, along with Ebenezer Pool and many other men and women who were players in Sandy Bay's history. The mossy headstones are only a few feet above the high-tide line, and the sound of the Old Sloop church bell still blends with the quiet waves.

Find Out More

I used many books in my search to learn how people in Sandy Bay lived in 1814. Three books in particular helped me understand the life of the fisherfolk and the sea.

Junger, Sebastian. *The Perfect Storm: A True Story of Men Against the Sea*. New York: HarperCollins Publishers, 1997. A thrilling true-life fishing adventure with a wealth of information on the Cape Ann fishery, both modern and historic.

Kipling, Rudyard. *Captains Courageous: A Story of the Grand Banks*. Garden City, NY: Sundial Press, 1931. First published in 1896. The greatest sea novel ever written, in my opinion, with characters so realistic that they all but jump off the page.

Kurlansky, Mark. *Cod: A Biography of the Fish That Changed the World*. New York: Penguin Putnam, 1997. A fascinating and complete history of—believe it or not—cod-fishing.

BIBLIOGRAPHY

Babson, John J. *History of Gloucester: The Town of Gloucester, Cape Ann, Including the Town of Rockport.* Gloucester, MA: Procter Brothers, 1860. A classic history of the famous seafaring town.

Benn, Carl. *The War of 1812.* Oxford, UK: Osprey Publishing, 2002. An overview of the War of 1812 from political and cultural points of view.

Bentley, William. *The Diary of William Bentley, D.D., Pastor of the East Church, Salem, Massachusetts.* Vol. 4, 1/1811–12/1814. Gloucester, MA: Peter Smith Publishers, 1962. Bentley was an eyewitness to the panic that hit coastal towns over the rumor of the British attacks.

Blake, Noah. *1805 Diary of an Early American Boy.* Commentary by Eric Sloane. New York: Ballantine Books, 1965. A rich source of information on early American household chores and tools.

Bonfanti, Leo. *Strange Beliefs, Customs, and Superstitions of New England.* New England Historical Series. Wakefield, MA: Pride Publications, 1980. Documentation of many historical traditions, including the belief that it was tempting fate for a fisherman to learn to swim.

Child, Lydia Maria. *The American Frugal Housewife.* Boston: Carter, Hendee, 1833. First published in 1828. A cookbook and housewife's guide "dedicated to those who are not ashamed of economy."

Clarke, William. *The Boy's Own Book: A Complete Encyclopedia of All the Diversions, Athletic, Scientific, and Recreative, of Boyhood and Youth.* Bedford, MA: Applewood Books, 1996. First printing 1829 by Monroe and Francis, Boston. The title says it all: what kids did before video games.

Coles, Harry L. *The War of 1812.* Chicago: University of Chicago Press, 1965. A study of the military operations of the war on land and sea.

Garland, Joseph E. *The Gloucester Guide: A Stroll Through Place and Time.* Rockport, MA: Protean Press, 1990. A guide to the buildings, streets, and other locations of Cape Ann history.

Hagelstein, Isabella. *New England's Colonial Architecture.* Lexington, MA: Primer Press, 1983. A description of mansions, cottages, and taverns.

Harrison, Nancy, and Woodward, Jean L. *Along the Coast of Essex County: A Guidebook.* Boston: The Junior League of Boston, 1970. A step-by-step investigation of historic sites and homes in Rockport (now Sandy Bay).

Hunt, Gaillard. *As We Were: Life in America, 1814.* Originally published in 1914 as *Life in America One Hundred Years Ago.* Stockbridge, MA: Berkshire House, 1993. An examination of New England life in the year 1814, the year of the invasion of Sandy Bay, with an emphasis on attitudes and social values.

BIBLIOGRAPHY

McLane, Merrill F. *Place Names of Old Sandy Bay, Rockport, Massachusetts.* Bethesda, MD: Helene Orbaen, 1998. A monograph on colonial and early American names of coves, islands, streets, and lighthouses in Sandy Bay.

Parsons, Eleanor. *Fish, Timber, Granite, and Gold: A Great Stone Wall on Cape Ann Leads to the Story of the Early Norwoods.* Rockport, MA: Sandy Bay Historical Society and Museums, 2003. Provides detailed street maps of Sandy Bay/Rockport.

Parsons, Eleanor. *Rockport: The Making of a Tourist Treasure.* Rockport, MA: Twin Lights Publishers, Inc., 1998. A history of the town of Sandy Bay, which changed its name to Rockport in the early 1800s.

Perley, Sidney. *Historic Storms of New England: Its Gales, Hurricanes, Tornadoes. ...* Beverly, MA: Commonwealth Editions, 2001. First published by Salem Press, Salem, Massachusetts, 1891. A chronicle of New England storms and how people reacted to them.

Platt, Richard. *Man of War.* Illustrated by Stephen Biesty. London: Dorling Kindersley, 1993. A meticulously illustrated guide to a British warship.

Pool, Calvin W. "Narrative of an Event in the History of Sandy Bay." *Rockport Review,* July 14, 1894. Calvin Pool interviewed the few surviving eyewitnesses of the event to create this account for the town newspaper. His handwritten original is preserved in the Sandy Bay Historical Society.

Pool, Ebenezer. *History of the Town of Rockport.* Rockport, MA: Rockport Review Office, 1888. An eyewitness account of the events in Sandy Bay in 1813 and 1814. Ebenezer Pool remained Sandy Bay's historian till his death sixty years after the invasion.

Pope, Eleanor. *The Wilds of Cape Ann: A Guide to the Natural Areas of Essex, Gloucester, Manchester, and Rockport, Massachusetts.* Boston, MA: Nimrod Press, 1981. A guide to the natural areas of Gloucester and Rockport.

Pringle, James R. *History of the Town and City of Gloucester, Cape Ann, Massachusetts.* Gloucester, MA: Ten Pound Island Book Co., 1997. First published in 1892. A detailed social and political history of Cape Ann.

Procter, George H. *The Fishermen's Memorial and Record Book.* Gloucester, MA: Procter Brothers, 1873. Details on North Atlantic vessels, fish, and fishing techniques.

Seymour, John. *Forgotten Household Crafts.* New York: Alfred A. Knopf, 1987. How to clean, cook, and sew using nineteenth-century methods.

Sloane, Eric. *Almanac and Weather Forecaster.* New York: Hawthorn Books, 1955. New England storms and weather lore.

BIBLIOGRAPHY

Sloane, Eric. *A Museum of Early American Tools*. New York: Ballantine Books, 1964. An illustrated listing of New England household implements.

Smith, John. *Captain John Smith's America: Selections from his Writings*. Edited by John Lankford. New York: Harper and Row, 1967. John Smith was perhaps the first European to describe Cape Ann, in 1614, and to comment on the incredible abundance of fish in the deep, cold waters.

Smith, Sylvanus. *Fisheries of Cape Ann*. Gloucester, MA: Press of Gloucester, 1915. Smith grew up in Sandy Bay and recounts his childhood memories of the town in the 1830s.

Swan, Marshall W. S. *Town on Sandy Bay: A History of Rockport, Massachusetts*. Canaan, NH: Phoenix Publishing, 1980. A history of the town and its founding families.

Thoreau, Henry David. *Cape Cod*. New York: Thomas Y. Crowell, 1961. First published in 1865. Thoreau's classic description of the landscape of New England, with many details about life in a fishing village in the nineteenth century.

Walder, David. *Nelson: A Biography*. New York: Dial Press / James Wade, 1978. Information on the conduct, deportment, and uniforms of British naval officers of the period.

Wright, Merideth. *Everyday Dress of Rural America, 1783–1800: With Instructions and Patterns*. New York: Dover Publications, 1990. Detailed descriptions of the clothing of New England men, women, and children of various social classes and occupations.

ACKNOWLEDGMENTS

I've spent many happy hours searching for the bones of Sandy Bay beneath the twenty-first-century trappings of Rockport, Massachusetts, and I'm grateful for all the help that I've had along the way.

The Sandy Bay Historical Society in Rockport preserves a wealth of history. I would like to thank Cynthia Peckham, curator of the society, who was generous in sharing her time and expertise. She showed me the treasures of the museum, including Ebenezer Pool's original manuscripts and even the cannonball that struck the church on the night of the invasion.

I found much helpful material thanks to Stephanie Buck at the Cape Ann Historical Museum, an invaluable resource for those interested in Cape Ann's rich history. Many thanks also to the hospitable staff at the Bethlehem Public Library in Delmar, New York, and the Amsterdam Free Library in Amsterdam, New York.

My sincere thanks to historian Joseph Balkoski, who was kind enough to read the manuscript and share his amazing knowledge of military history. He gave me many valuable suggestions and corrections. Any errors that remain are mine alone.

Thanks to Joan Jobson for her artwork and for reading the first chapter again and again—and again.

I am grateful to the Highlights Foundation for allowing me to attend the Novel Mentoring Workshop led by Carolyn Coman and Jane Resh Thomas, who guided the group of writers with passion and creativity. Jane never let me forget for a minute to keep looking into the hearts of the characters.

I am enormously indebted to Carolyn P. Yoder of Calkins Creek for working with me to develop *The Invasion of Sandy Bay*. Her patience was endless, and I deeply appreciate her creative and insightful editing.

Thanks to Alex Steele, my first and fiercest editor. His literary skills were essential to the development of this book, and I am grateful to him for sharing his talents with me.

Thanks to Timothy Steele for leading me up, down, and along the rocks of Bearskin Neck.

Thanks to my husband, George Steele, for ... everything.

I would like to offer a special tribute to my mother and father, Ann and Pedro Sanchez, who first loved Cape Ann and showed it to me. Thanks especially to my mother for waiting for me so many times as I sat on a rock and gazed out to sea.